# Cody swept Trisha into his arms

before she could step onto the soft ground. The next thing she knew, Trisha was being carried across the wet grass.

Never once had any man literally swept her off her feet and carried her as if she were some petite princess. She suddenly laughed for the sheer joy of it.

"So do you want to go to the party?" Trisha asked Cody as he stood her upright.

He lifted his hands and draped his forearms across her shoulders, his hands meeting under her tousled cascade of pale golden hair shimmering in the moonlight. The hard knuckles of his thumbs caressed her neck.

"Whatever you want, I want, too."

The hint of intimacy in his tone and words brought a shiver to Trisha's skin and reminded her of her earlier thought that there could be danger in a single evening with him.

And then she recklessly rejected the warning.

Dear Reader,

It's time to celebrate! This month we are thrilled to present our 1000th Silhouette Romance novel—*Regan's Pride*, written by one of your most beloved authors, Diana Palmer. This poignant love story is also the latest addition to her ever-popular LONG TALL TEXANS.

But that's just the start of CELEBRATION 1000! Throughout April, May, June and July we'll be bringing you wonderful romances by authors you've loved for years— Debbie Macomber, Tracy Sinclair and Annette Broadrick. And so many of your new favorites—Suzanne Carey, Laurie Paige, Marie Ferrarella and Elizabeth August.

This month, look for *Marry Me Again* by Suzanne Carey, an intriguing tale of marriage to an irresistible stranger.

The FABULOUS FATHERS continue with *A Father's Promise* by Helen R. Myers. Left to care all alone for his infant son, Big John Paladin sets out to win back the woman he once wronged.

Each month of our celebration we'll also present an author who is brand-new to Silhouette Romance. In April, Sandra Steffen debuts with an enchanting story, *Child of Her Dreams*.

Be sure to look for *The Bachelor Cure*, a delightful love story from the popular Pepper Adams. And don't miss the madcap romantic reunion in *Romancing Cody* by Rena McKay.

We've planned CELEBRATION 1000! for you, our wonderful readers. So, stake out your favorite easy chair and put a Do Not Disturb sign on the door. And get ready to fall in love all over again with Silhouette Romance.

Happy reading!

Anne Canadeo
Senior Editor
Silhouette Romance

Please address questions and book requests to:
Reader Service
U.S.: P.O. Box 1325, Buffalo, NY 14269
Canadian: P.O. Box 1050, Niagara Falls, Ont. L2E 7G7

# ROMANCING CODY

## Rena McKay

Silhouette
ROMANCE™
Published by Silhouette Books
America's Publisher of Contemporary Romance

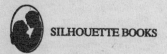

**SILHOUETTE BOOKS**

ISBN 0-373-19004-2

ROMANCING CODY

## RENA McKAY

currently lives in Oregon, and her novels reflect her love of travel. She's used her knowledge of places such as the American Southwest, Scotland and even Hawaii to create memorable settings for her stories. When she's not traveling, Rena likes reading, cats and long walks on the beach.

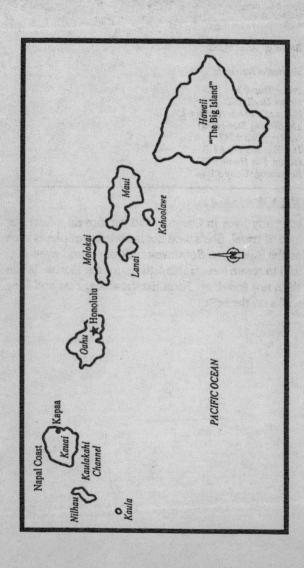

# *Chapter One*

"**W**ho invented class reunions, anyway?"

"Probably the same person who thought locking yourself in a cage full of hungry sharks would be a really fun thing to do," a disgruntled voice answered. "Have you noticed how people really enjoy seeing that a former cheerleader has put on a few pounds? I should have brought along a scale so they wouldn't have to speculate about how much I've gained."

The first voice laughed. "Speaking of weight... Have you seen Trisha Lassiter?"

"How could I miss her? That figure... the hair... and those *legs*. Jerry practically tripped over his eyeballs when he saw her in the registration line. Wait'll I get him home. I'm going to..."

The voices faded down the walkway on the other side of the tall hedge, so Trisha didn't hear what was going to happen to the unfortunate Jerry. She didn't recognize the voices, not surprising, because it had been ten years since she'd had any contact with her old classmates at Horton High. A former cheerleader could be any one of a dozen girls, all of whom had been cute, curvy and vivacious.

As opposed to Trisha herself, who in high school had been none of those things.

She reached into the rental car for her name tag and pinned it to her white tank top. Her old class yearbook lay on the seat, and she impulsively picked it up. Up front were the large photos of important graduates: valedictorian and salutatorian, class officers, the "Big Ten on Campus." None of which included her.

She paused at one of the "Big Ten" photos. There he was, the Heartthrob of Horton High. The haircut may be a little out·of-date now, but those darkly handsome good looks would never be. The black hair, looking as if a stray lock might fall across the tanned forehead at any moment. The dazzling smile that had sizzled the hormones of any teenage girl within range and sent fathers pacing the floor with anxiety. The bad-boy eyes, sexy and reckless and teasing, promising fun and excitement and delicious danger. And the black-and-white photo didn't even begin to reveal how blue those eyes were.

In her more foolish high school moments she had dreamily composed sappy descriptions of those eyes. Blue as a midnight mountain. Blue as a tropical lagoon. Lapis lazuli blue. She touched the photo with a fingertip, as she had, a few brief, incandescent times, touched that sensuous mouth with her own....

Then she had to laugh at herself. Such ridiculous adolescent fantasies of long ago.

Cody Malone probably wouldn't even remember her. Although he might. Could any guy forget the class whale, as she'd once heard herself cruelly described, furiously hitting him over the head with a several-pound book of the complete works of William Shakespeare?

She flipped through the yearbook to the smaller photos of the also-rans of Horton High. There she was. What had she weighed when that photo was taken? One-ninety-five? And her hair. She was always snipping at it back then, taking a little off here, a little off there, until in the photo it was almost a crewcut. On reflection, she had no idea why she was always cutting it. Unless, perhaps, frustrated with the hated pounds, she cut it just to get rid of some part of herself. If she couldn't take off weight, she could at least take off hair.

She felt an odd sort of sorrow for the hostile, defiant-looking girl forever trapped on those aging pages. Smile, she wanted to say to her; everything turned out fine, after all.

She turned a page and found the photo of Dawn Terrill, her best friend at Horton High, Dawn with her long dark hair and sweet smile. Seeing Dawn again was the primary reason she'd come to this reunion. They'd corresponded for a while after graduation, but then Dawn had married and moved back East, Trisha had made several moves and they'd just lost touch. She'd called the reunion committee chairman to make certain Dawn would be here. She'd briefly thought of trying to contact Dawn ahead of time, but her own reunion notice had arrived so late that she'd decided just to come and surprise her.

She followed the hedge to the gateway into the city park bordering the river that flowed through Horton. A banner strung between two trees identified the event as a tenth-year class reunion.

The park looked just as it always had, sloping lawn worn to bare dirt in places, spreading maple trees with an occasional pine soaring above, weathered picnic tables. She used to come here and read, back propped against a tree trunk, gaze sometimes lifting to Mount Shasta and the lesser mountains of northern California in the distance. Sometimes she'd daydreamed of a moment when she'd return to Horton, slim and beautiful and successful, and everyone would marvel at her. And be sorry at how they'd treated her.

Once more she had to laugh at herself, but her experience at the registration desk in the high school gym earlier today had indeed been gratifying. The first total lack of recognition. The double-take when she identified herself. The whispers that followed her as she made her way back to the gym entrance at the end of the line.

*That's really Trisha?*

*What'd she do, get a body transplant?*

She was wearing white shorts, which, afraid of snickers about fat thighs rubbing together like whale blubber, she'd never have done in high school. But now her legs were long

and slim and golden tan. Once she'd also been embarrassed
about her height, and had slumped to try to hide it, but now
she walked tall and self-confidently.

She rounded the corner of the covered picnic shelter, and
Angela Coulter, former yearbook editor, waved her over.
Angela Coulter Winters now, according to the name tag.

"Trisha, it's so nice you could come this year! I suppose
you've heard this a hundred times already, but you do look
fabulous. I understand you live in Hawaii now?"

"Yes. On the island of Kauai."

"What do you do there?" The slim blonde who spoke
had not been blond in high school, but Trisha didn't have to
glance at the name tag to identify her. Connie Melkin, who,
as editor of the school newspaper, had once turned down
Trisha's request to cover a local fashion show with the
comment that they needed someone "more sophisticated."
"More sophisticated" translating to "less fat," of course,
as if extra pounds somehow invalidated Trisha's fashion
judgment.

But that was all long in the past, she reminded herself
firmly.

"I do jewelry design and have a gift shop of my own. And
I model in an occasional fashion show. And you?" Trisha
tilted her head to include both women in the question.

Angela said that she worked in the local electric company office and was recently divorced from Mike Winters,
the guy she'd gone steady with all through high school.
"Connie here just dumped husband number three," she
added.

If the rather tart comment about husbands bothered
Connie, she didn't let on. "Keep trying until you get it right,
that's my motto," she said cheerfully. "I had one of my
honeymoons in Hawaii. Lucky you to *live* there. You're not
married?"

"No."

Trisha thought that might elicit a certain smugly conde-
scending response, something along the unspoken lines of,
She may *look* great, but she can't snag a *husband*.

But all that happened in response to Trisha's statement about her unmarried status was that Angela muttered, "Smart girl."

After Angela and Connie drifted off, Trisha circulated, something she'd never have done in the old days when she tended to hide in a corner...if she could find a corner large enough.

She asked several people about Dawn, but no one had seen her yet. Finally Trisha decided to inquire about Dawn at the table set up by the reunion committee to take care of those who hadn't arrived in time to register at the high school gym.

"Dawn Terrill Dalton?" repeated the woman, Blair Davis Barton, one of many who had completely failed to recognize Trisha when she'd registered earlier. The three-name system for identifying women by tacking on the married name was informative, but Trisha found it mildly disconcerting, as if they'd all sprouted an additional appendage. "I know we had an address for her. Her mother and Connie Melkin's mother were friends and kept in touch."

Brant Gordon, a football player who had turned into an insurance salesman, flipped through a clipboard sheaf of names and addresses. "Here it is. She paid her reunion fee a couple of months ago, but she hasn't shown up yet."

Trisha regretfully suspected that if Dawn hadn't arrived by now, she probably wasn't coming. Dawn had always been a very punctual person. Trisha jotted down Dawn's Minneapolis address and phone number, pleased to have that much in spite of her disappointment at not seeing her old friend.

"Terrific reunion, isn't it?" Brant Gordon's eyes roamed over her as if he were planning a touchdown strategy. "Are you coming to the dance with anyone tonight?"

Brant Gordon asking her, in a roundabout way, for a date? Trisha well remembered once colliding with him in a hallway at Horton High. He hadn't said anything rude or insulting; he simply hadn't seen her. One hundred and ninety-five pounds, and she was totally invisible to the likes of Brant Gordon. He might have collided with a post for all the notice he gave her.

She was tempted to remind him of the incident, perhaps shade her eyes and say tartly, "Is that a voice? Do I hear someone speaking?" But there was no point in being unpleasant just because of past hurt feelings. She was more mature than that, as she'd reminded herself numerous times on the long flight from Honolulu to San Francisco.

So all she did was say, in a bright way that tactfully dismissed Brant's question, "I'm really looking forward to seeing the new country club." But she wasn't quite mature enough, she had to admit, to keep from feeling just a tiny bit of satisfaction that Brant looked disappointed. And was also rapidly losing his hair.

"We have a good turnout this year," Blair said. "Only about half the class made it for the fifth-year reunion."

"I haven't seen Kathy Devere or Donna Haagstrom yet." She added another name as if it were an afterthought. Although it wasn't. "Or Cody Malone."

Blair's face lit up. It was Blair, of course, whom Cody had taken to the senior prom, roaring up to the school gym with her on the back of his battered old motorcycle. Blair's red hair was windblown, and grease speckled her off-the-shoulder gown, but almost every girl at Horton High would gladly have traded a designer gown, a limousine ride and probably several years of her life to be with a tux-clad Cody on that motorcycle.

These details of the prom were, however, all hearsay to Trisha. She and Dawn had spent senior-prom night playing a dart game with a photo of Cody as a target.

"We heard from Cody. He said he'd be here." Blair smiled and shook her head, like a tolerant mother resigned to her child's escapades. "But you know Cody. I remember one time he was supposed to take me to a movie, but he stood me up and took Barbara Turner to some stock-car races instead. I was devastated."

"So what did you do?" Trisha asked curiously, remembering a certain devastation of her own.

"Just pretended it never happened and practically broke down the front door getting to him the next time he came by and honked his motorcycle horn. Cody could get away with things like that." Blair sighed, but her smile was fondly reminiscent. Then her voice lowered to a conspiratorial pitch, and her eyes sparkled. "But my husband doesn't need to know any of this, of course!"

She nodded her head toward a guy lying on the grass under a nearby tree, and Trisha was surprised to see that he was at least twenty years older than Blair.

"Hey, remember the time Cody jumped his motorcycle over the concrete wall out by the track field?" Brant asked.

"And wound up in the hospital with so many girls visiting him that they practically needed a police officer to control the traffic in and out of his room." Blair laughed. "Oh, and remember that time he outran the police on his motorcycle, and then got caught because he stopped to help a girl with a flat tire?"

"So what's he doing now?" Trisha cut in. What Cody Malone had been, if they could get off this happy trail of juvenile memories, was a self-centered, irresponsible teenage jock, a rebel who broke rules and hearts with cavalier carelessness.

"His address is in Vancouver, Washington, but he didn't fill out the personal information sheet," Blair said.

Perhaps because he hadn't been able to sweet-talk some gullible woman into doing it for him, Trisha thought snidely.

A roar from the parking area suddenly rose above the buzz of reunion conversation.

"You don't suppose—" Blair's gaze darted to the opening in the hedge as an engine revved to fever pitch and then abruptly died.

It could be a motorcycle gang passing through, Trisha thought. But it wasn't.

Cody Malone strode through the gate as if he owned the park. Hair as thick as ever, stride just as jaunty, grin just as dazzling. Heavy black boots on his feet, faded jeans and T-shirt on a body that was as lean and athletic as it had always been. Trisha wasn't close enough to see his eyes, but she didn't need a face-to-face inspection to know they were fully as blue and sexy and teasing as they had been ten years ago. He lifted one arm in greeting and cries came from all over the park.

"Cody!"

"Hey, Cody, how many cops did you outrun today?"

"Malone!"

A wave flowed through the crowd as people moved toward him. Trisha didn't run and hide behind a tree as she might once have done, but she didn't join the welcoming wave.

There was much male backslapping and handshaking; there were as many female hugs. Trisha felt mildly scornful of all the attention heaped on Cody. From all appearances he might have spent the last ten years in a vacuum-packed can, just waiting for this moment to step forth.

Yet, as the crowd parted to let him make his way to the card table set up as registration desk, a disconcerting echo of the past jolted through her. Her new-and-improved legs astonished her with a distinct flutter in the knees, and her thoroughly mature heart unexpectedly pounded in an adolescent stampede of pulse. Now what was all *that* about? she wondered, annoyed with herself.

Blair greeted Cody with a big hug, her face animated as she personally pinned a name tag on him. Then people gathered around him again, and from the laughter and guffaws, Trisha knew the game of "Remember when—" was in full swing. Did anyone, she wondered, remind him of the time he had briefly dated the class whale...and how he had humiliated her?

Suddenly, in spite of her changed appearance and status, Trisha was momentarily on the outside looking in again. She had little to reminisce about with most of these people. She had never been a part of their pranks and parties and proms.

She had entered Horton High near the beginning of her senior year. Her father was a troubleshooter with a chain of hardware stores, frequently transferred to a new problem area, and they never lived anywhere for long. He was transferred again three months before her graduation, and she'd finished the year living with an elderly neighbor-couple so she wouldn't have to change schools again. Her first day at Horton High was forever branded in her memory as the day some boy snickered and muttered, "How'd she ever manage to get through the *door?*"

So why was she here, really?

Because she'd hoped to see Dawn, of course. But perhaps, to be honest, because she also wanted her old classmates to see that she was no longer the class whale. She hadn't, as she'd heard one whisper suggest, had a nose job or been liposuctioned from head to toe, but she'd done a thorough job on herself physically. She'd lost sixty pounds, and the one-thirty-five remaining was satisfactorily distributed on her five-foot-ten frame. She'd had her teeth straightened and wasn't self-conscious about smiling now. She'd stopped chopping off her hair, and it now hung to her shoulders in a shimmer of pale gold. She'd learned to walk with a regal posture—Hugh Lawton, a good friend had really nagged her on that!—and only modesty, not self-consciousness about her body, dictated the skimpiness of her bikinis. Several months ago, her photo, taken in a swimsuit at a fashion show, had appeared on the cover of a tourist brochure about Kauai.

Her shop, The Pink Turtle, was more gallery than the souvenir-type gift shop it had been when she bought it. The items on her shelves and in her display cases were handcrafted by some of the best artisans and craftsmen on the island, and she often had a waiting list of people wanting to buy the coral jewelry she designed and created. The Pink Turtle had several times been listed in travel magazines as a place to visit on the island.

She did have occasional minor relapses in both her self-confidence and sensible-eating habits, but for the most part she had put her overweight, unhappy past behind her. She was a different person now than the vulnerable, insecure girl who had been engulfed in a teenage crush that had hit with the power and intensity of a storm wave burying an unwary surfer.

*That's for me* had been her immediate reaction the first time she saw Cody Malone when he lazily strolled ten minutes late into her U.S. history class her second day at Horton High. The teacher, less susceptible to Cody's good looks and teenage charisma than Trisha, immediately sent him to the office for a tardy slip. From the doorway he turned and flashed a dazzling grin. Eventually she'd realized that grin had been for everyone, but at the moment she'd thought it

was just for her. Her palms grew damp, her throat dry and
her equilibrium fluttery. The fervent thought repeated itself. *That's for me.*

She hadn't thought of her feelings for him as a crush back
then, of course. She was positive she was madly in love, and
her feelings had certainly lasted far longer than most fleet-
ing teenage crushes.

An unexpected thought alarmed her enough to make her
choke on the root beer she was drinking as she stood in line
for the barbecued-chicken dinner. Hidden under her other
reasons for attending the reunion, was there some subcon-
scious urge to ignite the flames on a new relationship with
Cody Malone?

No. Definitely not, she assured herself. Cody was the kind
of guy you had a wild crush on in high school, not one with
whom you got involved with as an adult. The qualities that
were wickedly attractive in a teenage boy weren't the same
ones that made for success in a mature relationship.

In high school, faithfulness and commitment were as
foreign to Cody as wearing high heels had been to her. He
never went steady, just sampled girls like a hearty eater
sampling desserts at a loaded buffet. And, from what little
she'd seen so far, she saw no reason to believe he'd changed.
He still projected a reckless virility and audacious sexiness.
And he was probably still, married or not, cutting a wide
swath across female hearts.

Cody was still standing in line when Trisha found an
empty spot at a picnic table. She glanced up, and for a moment their eyes met. He looked puzzled, and then his head
gave a small backward jerk of surprise, as if he had just
recognized her.

Trisha welcomed the reason to look away as a short,
plump woman plopped down beside her on the picnic
bench. Her name tag read Candace Amark Williams, which
momentarily left Trisha blank.

"Remember me? Candy, the cheerleader who was always the one on top when we did pyramids?" The information and the voice identified her as the woman Trisha had
overheard talking by the hedge. "Although it would prob-

ably take a crane to lift me now," Candy added with a self-deprecating sigh.

Actually, although the face was rounder and the curves more ample, Candy was still cute and sparkly. Trisha also remembered that the only times Candy had ever spoken to her at Horton High were when she needed information about some class assignment she'd missed because she was too busy flirting or cheerleading.

Once more Trisha reminded herself of her decision to forget past snubs and injustices, so with all the warmth she could muster, she said, "We had a bookkeeping class together, I believe."

"What we're all dying to know, of course, is how did you do it? Every time I lose five pounds, I gain back ten."

"I guess I tried every diet in existence," Trisha admitted. Ruefully she listed a few of them. "Grape diet, grapefruit diet, pasta diet, mushroom diet. Carbohydrate diets and protein diets and just plain starve-yourself diets. And I started a lot of different exercise programs." She'd start some intense program of aerobics, jogging and swimming, but, sore both physically and mentally, would give it up as impossible after the first week.

"So what worked?"

"Well—" It was such a long, involved story. It was also something she doubted she could have accomplished without Hugh Lawton's faith and encouragement.

"Oh, no," Candy wailed. "You're going to tell me it all came down to willpower." She laughed. "Oh, well. Fortunately, Jerry says he likes me a little plump, anyway. See you at the dance tonight, okay?"

Trisha smiled and nodded, but unexpectedly she bumped into a feeling she hadn't anticipated, a definite twinge of resentment that nearly everyone was being so friendly and nice to her now. Appearance shouldn't make that much difference. Would it have killed them to be a little nicer to her ten years ago when it really mattered?

Her gaze roamed the scattered tables and found Cody just swinging a leg over a bench at a trio of picnic tables shoved together in a horseshoe arrangement. The jock crowd, old athletes gathering to share tales of their glory days. And

Cody had the most glory of all to recall, of course. Foot-ball-team captain, wrestling star, Winter Prom King. And undisputed champion in the sport of girl chasing...or being chased.

She watched Cody walk over to the big metal can filled with soft drinks and beer packed in ice. The August day was hot, and perspiration blotched the back of his plain white T-shirt. The fabric clung to his chest and shoulders, rippling slightly with the movement of muscles as he leaned over and rummaged in the metal can.

She checked out another portion of his physique, remembering a giggling Candy once saying that he had "buns that make you want to just grab hold and squeeze." She also remembered being shocked at the time, because it had never occurred to her, even in her wildest teenage fantasies, to grab any portion of Cody's anatomy, and most certainly not *that* portion.

But, if one wanted to be crude, she decided as he leaned farther over the metal can, he definitely had grabbable buns.

Suddenly, his old prom date Blair darted up, grabbed a chunk of ice from the barrel and shoved it down the back of his T-shirt. He looked momentarily startled but quickly retaliated by grabbing her around the waist and swabbing the back of her neck with more ice. She squealed and twisted in phony panic, and a scoop of ice cream flew out of somewhere and landed on Cody's back. Two guys ran for the barrel and it went down when they collided, ice and soft drinks and beer cans rolling in all directions. A woman dashed up and gleefully planted a handful of barbecue sauce on one man's neck. Someone grabbed a can of beer and sprayed everyone within reach.

Trisha stared in disbelief as within the space of a few seconds a reasonably dignified gathering turned into a wild melee. It took only about five more seconds for her to decide she was leaving. Of all the ridiculous, juvenile, idiotic... Good Lord, they were adults now, not a herd of food-fighting adolescents. She headed for her car.

She got no farther than the nearest ice-cream puddle before someone slammed into her, tumbling her sideways to the ground. When she got her head straight, she realized it was that clod Brant Gordon, the very same person who had once collided with her in the hallway of Horton High and hadn't even acknowledged her existence.

He was not getting away with it this time, she vowed furiously. Fueled by all the old frustration and anger that she'd carefully held in check so far, she grabbed a handful of melting ice cream and mashed it into the back of Brant's thinning hair.

Hey, she thought, surprised, that felt good! She wiped her hands on her stained shorts and found another target as the food fight escalated around her. Gleefully, she paid back a few wrongs of the past. Candy Amark, snubbing her in high school, now wanting diet secrets. Doug Timmons, a football player who'd taken her out, she later learned, because someone had dared him to date a girl who weighed as much as he did. A squirt of root beer for Connie Melkin, a smear of chocolate syrup for that guy who'd made the too-big-for-the-door crack on her first day at Horton High.

But enough was enough. She caught her breath behind an overturned picnic table and then made a dash for the opening in the hedge. But before she could reach it, a tide of moving bodies engulfed her. Down she went again.

The pile of tangled arms and legs was only partially unwound when a shrill whistle sounded over the shrieks and yells. Silence fell as everyone suddenly realized the law had arrived. The law in the form of Officer Andy Harbeck, with whom more than one member of this graduating class had crossed paths in years gone by. He stepped between puddles of melting ice cream, eyed the banner and surveyed the crowd. "Oh, yes," he said in an ominous tone, "I remember this class."

The body weighing Trisha down slithered away, and she wiped a hand across her face. It came away covered with barbecue sauce. She wiped the sloppy mess on a denim-covered leg.

It was also then that she realized the leg belonged to a body that was still under her, that her breasts were flattened against a stained T-shirt. With an awful sense of premonition, she slowly raised herself and turned her head.

And there were those incredibly blue eyes she had once worshipped from afar.

Cody lifted his head as the hand on his chest skidded on a smear of chocolate sauce and tangled in his chest hair. He'd noticed her earlier while he was waiting in line for dinner. With her spectacular change in physical appearance it had taken a moment for recognition to sink in, but he'd known it was her. He'd briefly thought about going over to say hi but rejected the idea. He doubted she was eager to reminisce with him about old times at Horton High.

"Well, if it isn't Trisha Lassiter." He smiled ruefully. No point in trying to pretend they'd parted friends. "I suppose I should be grateful that this time you're not armed with a ten-pound volume of William Shakespeare."

She had barbecue sauce on her face and smears of chocolate sauce on her bottom, neither of which did anything to detract from the dazzling effect of her high-cheekboned face, lush hair and long legs. She scooted away from him so fast that she stuck her knee in a puddle of melting ice cream. He dug a handkerchief out of the rear pocket of his jeans and silently handed it to her.

She momentarily looked as if she might be going to tell him what he could do with his handkerchief, but she finally accepted it and dabbed at the knee. "Thank you."

Officer Harbeck's voice boomed across the park, chastising the class for their behavior. A well-earned chastising, Cody had to admit. Melting ice cream and trickling cans littered the ground, along with paper plates scattered like miniature flying saucers. The officer, with an impressive memory for names and faces, strolled among these now-overage students, scowling as he reminded various class members of youthful indiscretions. He stopped short when his shadow fell across Cody, something he had not done with any of the others.

"Cody Malone." It sounded more like an accusation than simple identification. "Seventy-six Harley-Davidson. I gave you more speeding tickets in a certain six-month period than I've ever given anyone before or since. And those were only the times I was able to catch you."

Cody was glad his eight-year-old niece Debbie was not here to hear this. She'd really give him a bad time about it. "I had a little problem with speed back then," he admitted.

"A *little* problem?" the officer challenged.

Cody grinned guiltily, and he wasn't surprised to see the beginnings of an answering smile add a new set of wrinkles to the officer's weatherbeaten old face. They'd been halfway friends in spite of all Cody's misdeeds. But the smile stopped before it became full-blown, as if the officer thought it improper to smile at an old adversary under these circumstances.

"As I recall, you occasionally did some community-service work as part of your punishment. Including cleanup work here in the park. I suggest you do it again now." Officer Harbeck swiveled to look at the now-silent and motionless crowd. "The rest of you can help. I'll be back in exactly sixty minutes, and I expect this park to be as spotless as your mother's tablecloth when company is coming. If it isn't—"

He didn't complete the threat, but everyone jumped into the cleanup work. Cody drained cans and stuffed them into a plastic bag. Trisha gathered paper plates and stray napkins, and their paths crossed several times over the next half hour. She didn't look his way but he wasn't certain if she was deliberately ignoring him or was simply unaware of him. Maybe she didn't even remember him. There were people here he had to admit he didn't remember.

No, she remembered him. She'd been too hurt and humiliated not to. He hadn't spent the last ten years agonizing over what he'd done to Trisha, but he'd thought about her a few times and wished he hadn't done it.

The next time their paths crossed, he stuck out an arm and stopped her.

# Chapter Two

"Oh, I'm sorry, I forgot. Your handkerchief." Trisha pulled the stained handkerchief from the pocket of her shorts. "I'll wash it at the motel and then see that it's returned to you."

"No, I'm not worried about my handkerchief." He stuffed the handkerchief in the rear pocket of his jeans, next to the corner of the sticky T-shirt he'd removed. He could feel sweat making dark swirls on his bare chest and trickling under the belt of his jeans. "It's a little late, about ten years late, in fact, but I want to apologize."

Her eyes flicked over him, and there was only a brief moment of delay before she said, "Apology accepted." Her tone was pleasant but impersonal. She did not take the opportunity to indulge in angry recriminations, but neither did she pretend coy ignorance about what the apology was for. She simply accepted it with poised dignity.

"For whatever it's worth, I never deliberately intended to hurt or humiliate you. I was just a...jerk. And I am sorry."

"There's no need to explain. If you'll excuse me, I see another paper plate over there—"

"Wait a minute." He reached out and snagged her arm again. "What have you been doing for the past ten years? Where do you live?"

The personal history she gave him was too fleshless even to qualify as skeletal. It consisted of the single statement that she lived on the Hawaiian island of Kauai and owned a gallery/gift shop called The Pink Turtle. His gaze ran down her slim body and back to her lush hair and elegant cheekbones no longer hidden under plump pillows of flesh. There was more than that to tell, he was certain, but she obviously didn't intend to elaborate. She didn't mention her marital status, but her name tag indicated her last name was still Lassiter, and she wasn't wearing a wedding ring.

"Did you move to Hawaii before or after the ... metamorphosis?"

"Before. Although I took a plane. I didn't swim with the other whales." The golden flecks in her hazel eyes sparked, and her tone was tart this time, but it wasn't nearly as impersonal.

He laughed, again ruefully. "Kids can be thoughtless."

"Cruel."

He nodded. "It takes a strong and determined person to make the changes you have. I admire that. It's also generous of you not to hold grudges, to come back and be so nice to everyone."

He'd known she had a thing going for him back then. He got teased about it occasionally, such gibes as "Hey, Cody, here comes your pet whale," or "Better run, Cody, she's looking at you like you're a banana split." And he'd deliberately taken advantage of those feelings. She'd been more fun than he expected, but it was a different kind of fun than he tended to look for in a girl in those days. She had other traits that he could now also look back on and appreciate. She was honest and direct, bright, funny, self-sufficient, loyal. But he hadn't been the kind of guy to give much thought to such valuable traits ten years ago.

"It was all a long time ago." Her mouth twitched in a hint of a smile. "Although I did pay back some old debts and get rid of a few lingering hostilities in the food fight. And what have you been doing for the past ten years?" He couldn't tell if she was really interested or asking just for the sake of politeness.

He suddenly remembered something. "Hey, I have a question for you."

"Question?" she repeated warily.

"How many psychiatrists does it take to change a light bulb?"

He saw the momentary widening of her eyes and knew she was surprised that he remembered that back in their brief relationship they'd exchanged silly knock-knock and light-bulb jokes.

With a reluctant smile, she said, "I don't know. How many psychiatrists *does* it take to change a light bulb?"

He leaned against the end of a picnic table, legs stretched out in front of him, feet crossed at the ankles. "Three. One to screw in the bulb, one to counsel the bulb about whether it really wants to change and one to give it therapy afterward to deal with the change."

She groaned and laughed at the same time. "That is terrible. That is the worst joke I've ever heard."

He'd forgotten what a wonderful laugh she had. And how easily laughter came to her after they'd dated a couple of times, because she'd so seldom even smiled at school.

Now his mouth turned downward in pretended hurt at the criticism, but he grinned, too. "Okay, so I'm not a stand-up comedian. I'm a volcanologist."

"You work with *volcanoes?*" she asked, her astonishment obvious.

"I'm glad you know what a volcanologist is. Sometimes, people seem to think it means I'm mixed up in some weird cult."

A yell interrupted the conversation. Reluctantly he took his eyes off Trisha. Candy, holding a green hose, repeated her loud demand that he help her hose down the puddles of melting ice cream.

"Okay, in a minute," he called back. On sudden impulse, he said to Trisha, "Look, if you don't already have plans for the dance tonight, would you like to go with me?"

For a moment, it was the old vulnerable Trisha peering out of those gold-flecked hazel eyes, and in the taut silence that followed, he knew she was remembering in harsher detail that spring of their senior year ten years ago.

He'd been close to flunking his English literature class. In fact, if he flunked it, he wouldn't have enough credits to graduate. But when the teacher assigned each class member the writing of a thousand-word paper on a Shakespearean play, he didn't just get busy and do it, as he should have. Instead, he decided to get Trisha Lassiter, who'd done a paper the previous quarter that the teacher had used as a glowing example of what she'd like to see, to do it for him. He took her to a couple of movies and then casually mentioned that he had this terrible problem with the Shakespearean paper. He wasn't troubled by guilt for dating her with an ulterior motive in mind; girls had always helped him with schoolwork when he was too busy with sports... or raising hell... to do it.

He'd strung her along for several more dates while she worked on the paper. They went canoeing on the river one time, and she always made brownies or cookies for study dates in her kitchen. Once, she fixed fried chicken for a picnic, although they had to walk to the park because his motorcycle was a basket case at the time. He hadn't given any thought to what would happen after she finished the paper, which was typical of his careless outlook on life back then. But he hadn't deliberately planned to do anything mean or humiliating to her. Which didn't excuse what had happened.

Several times he'd invited Trisha to sit with him at what was informally designated the VIP table in the school cafeteria, but he didn't really notice that she wasn't there when he arrived late one lunch period. He got the usual greetings, a "Yo, Cody," and a "How's it going, man?" as he walked from the lunch line over to the table. Then someone asked him, "Hey, Cody, you gonna race that dude from Danville tonight? He's telling everyone his Honda will leave you spinning in the dust."

He'd finished putting his Harley back together the previous evening, but he shook his head. "I have to take Trisha to a movie. She hasn't finished that paper for English lit for me yet."

There were frantic motions toward the divider that separated the main part of the cafeteria from the narrow area
where the kids scraped and stacked their dishes. It finally
dawned on him what all the silent pointing and rolling of
eyes was about, but not before his friend Bud Galeston, who
considered himself a great wit, spoke.

"Cody says he doesn't mind taking Trisha to the movies
so she'll do the paper for him, but he damn sure wishes
they'd quit charging him double just because she fills up two
seats. But he says that getting her in *one* seat is like trying to
stuff a whale into a phone booth."

The next sound was a crash from behind the divider. He
dashed around it and saw the smashed plate on the floor, the
door swinging in silent accusation. He tried to find her, but
she apparently fled the school grounds immediately.

He hadn't made either of those dumb statements; they
were Bud's crude idea of humor. But he *had* dated her to get
her to write the paper for him, and now she knew it. As did
everyone else at Horton High, because the story flew around
the hallways and classrooms like a ricocheting missile, col-
lecting new fat jokes at every turn. Ever the arrogant jerk,
however, he went over to her house that evening thinking he
could sweet-talk her out of her anger and salvage the paper
he still needed. But she'd surprised him with that spitfire
attack with the book, and he'd retreated in astonishment.

He shouldn't have dropped it there, of course. He should
have gone back, apologized and told her to forget the damn
paper. He should also have squelched the cruel snickers and
gossip by inviting her to the senior prom, which he knew
she'd been hoping he'd do. But he didn't do that. He just felt
unfairly put upon because he had to write the paper himself. Then he'd asked someone else, he couldn't even remember who now, to the prom.

The sensitivity of a brick, he thought ruefully.

Trisha broke the long silence between them with a blunt
question. "Unfortunately, men's name tags aren't as informative as women's. Are you married?"

"Would I be asking you to the dance if I were?"

"That's what I'm wondering."

Okay, fair enough. He hadn't exactly been noted for faithfulness or commitment back in his wilder days. He'd been known to take one girl out and palm her off on a dateless friend so he could take a different girl home. He sometimes wondered now why the hell they'd let him get away with stuff like that. Perhaps a few more girls should have reacted to his misdeeds as Trisha had, by clobbering him about the head and shoulders with a heavy object.

"No, I'm not married. Never married, in fact."

Another direct question, this one more like a challenge. "Would you be inviting me to the dance if I still looked the way I did ten years ago?"

"I don't know," he admitted honestly. "I like to think I'm not as shallow as I once was. My character back then had all the depth of an inkblot—"

"Or a lipstick smear," she agreed tartly. "You collected girls as if they were ornaments for your motorcycle. You regarded studies as if they were an unfair imposition on your social and athletic life."

Not a complimentary assessment, but unfortunately quite accurate.

A rain of spray from the hose Candy was holding suddenly drenched both of them. "Hey, I'm waiting," Candy yelled. Apparently, she wasn't ready to let the afternoon's foolishness end.

"Your fan club calls," Trisha murmured.

Another barrage of cold water rained down on them.

"I guess I'd better go help her before she drowns us. Look, we'll talk about the dance later, okay? After Officer Harbeck gets back and okays our cleanup job."

But when everything was finished, he couldn't find her. He checked the sandy beach and the parking lot, but she was definitely gone. He had no idea where she was staying.

Maybe she was trying to tell him something with her absence. That she already had plans for the dance. Or that she just didn't want to go with him. He was probably lucky, he thought wryly, that she was too much of a lady to suggest he take a flying leap into one of his volcanoes.

* * *

He rented a motel room, showered and changed out of the jeans with a handprint in barbecue sauce on the rear. He had to hang his suit—wrinkled from being folded in the luggage box of the seldom-used motorcycle—over steaming water in the bathtub to get it in shape for the reunion dance.

He snapped on the TV, watched a few minutes of some golf game and restlessly turned it off. He glanced at his watch. Blair and her husband had invited him over for predance cocktails, but the prospect didn't appeal to him. Connie Melkin was supposed to be there, and she'd been careful to let him know she was single now, but that didn't interest him, either.

What interested him was Trisha, and what he wanted was to go to the reunion dance with her.

And Cody Malone was the kind of man who went after what he wanted.

As she finished scrubbing the last picnic table, Trisha was still trying to decide how she should respond to Cody's invitation. Accepting his apology had been easy enough; no involvement was required. But the dance was a different matter.

She certainly didn't feel about him now as she had ten years ago. No breathless tightening in her chest, no incriminating blushes, no romantic fantasies of moonlight and kisses. Yet, after talking to him, laughing at his silly joke and feeling the impact of his grin and the approving warmth in his blue eyes, she was potently aware that she wasn't necessarily invulnerable to his charms even now. So going to the dance with him could be not only foolish but dangerous. What she did not need was an inappropriate recycling of some teenage infatuation.

But Cody apparently wasn't the same guy he'd been in high school. A man didn't become a volcanologist without considerable effort and determination. He'd also realized he owed her an apology and handled it gracefully. Was it fair to judge a man on who he'd been and what he'd done a decade ago?

Soon, the park, if not spotless as a mother's tablecloth, was clean enough to pass Officer Harbeck's inspection. Trisha, still undecided about the dance, looked around for Cody. A sudden shriek drew her attention to the class banner strung between two trees.

Cody and a couple of other guys were lifting a woman up to untie the banner. She balanced on Cody's shoulders, his hands on her ankles steadying her as she gave off more shrieks and squeals. When the banner came down, so did she, tumbling into Cody's waiting arms with yet another happy squeal.

Some things never change, Trisha thought wryly as she left the park. Cody and females were inseparable. Something she'd heard or read popped into her head: a reformed Don Juan makes the best husband. The small inner voice that sometimes spoke to her had a retort for that: but it's so damned hard to reform one. The fact that he'd never married didn't surprise her. The agile and wily Cody Malone trapped with a wedding ring? No way. By now, he'd probably forgotten he'd even mentioned the dance to her.

Back at her motel room, she stripped and headed directly for the shower. While she was shampooing her hair, she seriously considered skipping the dance. She'd accomplished her purpose here. She had a new address for Dawn and she'd satisfactorily astonished her former classmates. She'd even gotten the unexpected bonus of ridding herself of some old, buried hostilities in the food fight. So there was really no point in going to the dance.

The dance could well be, in fact, an embarrassing letdown. Perhaps no one would dance with her. Perhaps she'd be left standing alone in a dark corner.

She paused in the process of blow-drying her hair. Wasn't that one strand a little longer than the rest? Maybe she should snip just a little off—

*Cut it out,* Trisha commanded herself sternly as she eyed her reflection in the mirror. That was the old, insecure Trisha Lassiter talking, the old Trisha nervously snipping at her hair. The new Trisha isn't afraid to take a few chances. And she *is* going to the dance.

She lay down to nap for a few minutes after her hair was dry. The ringing phone woke her. She ran one hand through her hair, trying to unmuddle her head, and groped for the phone with the other hand.

"Hello?"

"I couldn't find you after the cleanup work in the park was finished."

The voice brought her instantly awake. He didn't identify himself, but she recognized his voice from the first word. Then the fact that he hadn't identified himself mildly piqued her. What an ego, to assume any female from Horton High would instantly know his voice.

"This is—?" she asked in her most distantly polite tone.

"Cody." She heard a hint of smile in his voice, as if he suspected she was deliberately putting him in his place. Gently making fun of her, he elaborately added, "Cody *Malone*."

"How did you know where I'm staying?"

"I didn't. I just started calling motels until I found one that said you were registered there. I'd have found you quicker if you'd stayed at the Arbor Inn rather than the Victorian Lodge."

The fact that he'd gone to that much trouble to locate her was momentarily flattering. Then she reminded herself that calling every motel in small-town Horton was not exactly a mind-boggling task.

"We didn't have a chance to discuss the dance again. I'm still hoping you'll go with me."

Trisha squeezed her eyes shut, her mind somersaulting back to a time when she'd have pushed a peanut with her nose the full length of Horton's main street just to hear those words.

Her palm suddenly went damp and slick against the receiver. Her teenage crush on Cody may have been foolish and misguided, but the feelings had been more intense and powerful than any she'd known since. It would be utter foolishness to risk involvement with the guy who had already broken her heart once.

*Oh, come on now,* some more sensible part of her scoffed. *Don't make such a big deal out of this. He isn't suggesting a red-hot affair, just a reunion dance.* After all, Cody lived on the mainland and she in Hawaii, and they'd never even see each other again unless they both happened to attend the twentieth reunion. So there was no good reason *not* to go with him.

But was there any good reason to *accept* the invitation?

Yes! The answer popped up like a metal duck at a carnival shooting gallery. Going to the dance with him would put a punctuation mark on the past.

That was it. The unhappy, overweight, insecure era of her life was over, but there had never been anything official to mark its end. What better way to signify an ending than a reunion dance with Cody Malone? And why not do it with a flourish! Suddenly, she felt giddy and a little reckless.

"I'll go with you on one condition."

Small pause as he apparently considered the possibilities. "And that is—?"

"We go on your motorcycle."

Riding behind Cody on his motorcycle where everyone could see that you were the chosen one had been one of the more gaudy elements of her teenage dreams, a fantasy she'd been cheated out of even during their brief relationship because the motorcycle had temporarily been a basket case of parts on his dining room table.

Now, frivolous as arriving at a dance on a motorcycle with Cody was at this adult stage of her life, it would also be the perfect means to closing out that old era.

"The motorcycle is a bit impractical in evening clothes. How about a taxi tonight, and we'll take a ride on the motorcycle tomorrow?"

"No. No taxi."

Another small pause as if he were considering reminding her that this was *Cody Malone,* and Cody, not the fortunate female he was honoring with his attentions, set the conditions. But all he said was a cheerful, "Very well, the motorcycle it is. I'll pick you up about eight-thirty?"

"Fine. I'll meet you in the lobby."

Trisha did her makeup and hair with more care than if she were about to step out on a runway at a fashion show in the

most luxurious hotel on Kauai. Then she eyed with some
doubt the dress she had brought for this evening. It was on
loan from Moori, the Hawaiian-born designer for whom she
usually modeled. She often wore daring designs in fashion
shows, but her personal wardrobe tended to be more conservative. But both Moori and Leslie, her roommate on the
island, had insisted she needed a knock-'em-dead design for
the reunion, and this dress was definitely in that category.

The front opening was a wide V, cut low enough to flirt
with a generous glimpse of cleavage, and the back was bare
all the way to the belt that nipped her waist. The skirt was
short and swingy, perfect for dancing. The color was what
Leslie called bad-girl red, as were her barely-there high-
heeled sandals.

Cody, she suspected, would love it.

She added jewelry of her own design and creation, slim,
dangling earrings of polished black coral, plus an elegant
pendant necklace of the same material.

It was through her jewelry designs that she had started
modeling with Moori. With the idea that it would be good
publicity for The Pink Turtle, she had taken several neck-
laces and earrings to Moori and asked if the designer would
be interested in having her models wear the jewelry as ac-
cessories in a fashion show. Yes, Moori was interested. She
also looked Trisha over and suggested she fill in for another model who was ill. Trisha had modeled occasionally
for her ever since.

She dabbed on perfume and then stepped back to survey
the overall results in the mirror.

Not the class whale.

She intended to get to the motel lobby before Cody arrived, to give her a few moments to steady her nerves, which
had unexpectedly turned almost as jittery as they had been
on her first teenage date with him. But he was already there,
rising from a chair to meet her as soon as she came through
the door. He didn't actually circle her like a predator sizing
up prey, but his eyes were definitely on the prowl.

"I want to tell you that you look beautiful...gor-
geous...fantastic...but actually I'm almost speech-
less."

Trisha managed to smile and say, "I'd say you're doing rather nicely." She felt dangerously light-headed, as if she had whirled into one of her more extravagant fantasies of long ago. Those prowling blue eyes said even more than his mouth, unspoken words that, ten years ago, she would have climbed mountains and swum rivers for. And that she had to admit were not unwelcome even now.

Cody was wearing a charcoal-colored suit, white shirt and a black tie with narrow diagonal stripes of dark red. He had been wickedly attractive as a brash teenage heartthrob, dangerously sexy in faded jeans and T-shirt this afternoon. At this moment, he was still wickedly attractive and dangerously sexy, but added to those qualities was the even more formidable appeal of a mature male.

He took her left hand in his. "Surely you don't really want to ride on the motorcycle," he protested. "I can still call a taxi—"

"We made a deal, remember?"

"So we did."

He eyed her speculatively, as if wondering what was behind her odd insistence on the motorcycle, but he didn't ask questions.

When they went outside, she was expecting to see the same beat-up old Harley, although she immediately realized that was illogical, of course. That noisy machine had no doubt long since collapsed in some junkyard. The girls had always complained about its hard, narrow seat, saying riding that motorcycle seat was like trying to balance on a broomstick; but everyone knew the complaints were really disguised bragging, a way of announcing, *Hey, look at me! I've been riding Cody's motorcycle!*

This sleek machine gleamed in the evening dusk, a metallic silver-gray, with matching saddlebags and a large luggage box. The double, padded seat was generously curved to fit both driver and passenger. Cody opened the luggage box and handed Trisha a helmet that matched the silver-gray of the motorcycle. His helmet was hanging on the handlebars.

Suddenly, he slipped an arm around her waist and pulled her close. She felt the strength of the arm and the hard muscles of his thigh against hers.

"We got off to a bad start ten years ago. Let's make this the kind of date we should have had way back then." For a moment, she thought he was going to kiss her. It was in the blue-smoke softness of his eyes. But all he did was touch a fingertip to the corner of her lips and slowly trace the upper curve. "Okay?" he whispered.

"Okay," she agreed, trying to sound less shaky than she felt. Perhaps her initial instinct not to risk even minuscule involvement with Cody had been the right one.

Punctuation mark, she reminded herself firmly. That's all Cody and this dance represented, a punctuation mark on the past.

He slipped his helmet on and then helped Trisha with hers. It covered most of her face, and she could feel her hairdo flattening against her head.

"Do I have to wear this?"

"Yep."

"I don't remember your ever using a helmet." Neither were his girlfriends encumbered with them. And, oh, how she'd envied those carefree girls with their hair blowing in the wind, their arms wrapped around Cody!

"I do a lot of things differently than I did ten years ago."

Okay, adjust the fantasy, she decided. No hair streaming in the wind.

Getting on the motorcycle in the full-skirted dress was not complicated, but neither was it exactly ladylike. The maneuver exposed a considerable amount of leg, which did not escape Cody's attention. Nor that of a guy just getting out of a Corvette in the parking area. She suspected the scarlet-lady dress and high heels tangled in motorcycle chrome looked like something out of a bad biker movie, but it was too late to change her mind now. She scrunched the full skirt into a frothy pile between her legs and clamped her knees to hold it there. She didn't know quite what to do with her hands and finally clasped her fingers lightly around Cody's waist.

For the first few minutes, she felt vulnerably exposed to
the cars zipping past her knees and uncomfortably aware of
the hard pavement rushing by only a few inches below her
feet, but then she began to relax and enjoy the ride. Cody
was neither speeding nor taking dangerous chances. She
wasn't quite certain when it happened, but her arms were all
the way around him now, and there was something deliciously sensual about leaning into the curves as the motorcycle glided around a corner, her body one with Cody and
the sleek machine.

At the country club, where other couples were arriving in
more conventional vehicles, everyone turned to look when
Cody and Trisha roared up. Trisha's dismount from the
motorcycle drew more male attention than she was comfortable with, but Cody just grinned at her. She did what she
could with her hair by running her fingers through it, and
Cody's appreciative glance told her that was enough.

"You two look like something out of an ad for the good
life," Blair observed. She sounded a little grumpy about it.
"Have you kept in touch over the years?"

"No," Cody said, adding meaningfully, "but that may
change."

And Trisha was uncertain if the shiver that suddenly
hopscotched up her spine represented apprehension or an-
ticipation.

The interior of the building was modest by country-club
standards, a horseshoe-shaped bar with dance floor on one
side and small tables on the other, but the exterior doors had
been opened to add the patio area for dancing. Lanterns
flickering on tall poles in the evening breeze outlined the
patio, and streamers and balloons decorated the interior.
The banner from the park hung across the end wall of the
dance area. Everyone seemed in good-humored but rela-
tively docile spirits, which Trisha took as an optimistic sign
that the dance would not go the way of the afternoon picnic.

"Drink?" Cody asked.

"White wine spritzer, please."

She waited off to one side while he worked his way
through the crowd at the bar to get the drinks. Several peo-

ple stopped to talk. The news that she had arrived with Cody
had apparently circulated with the speed that only light and
gossip can achieve, and what surprised Trisha was that no
one seemed surprised by it. She heard "you and Cody"
several times, as if they were regarded as an accepted couple.

When Cody returned with drinks in hand, someone yelled
and waved from a group crowded around two tables pushed
together. "Hey, Cody, over here!"

The tables looked full, but space emerged to make room
for two more chairs for Cody and Trisha. Cody, Trisha suspected, was the kind of guy for whom space would always
emerge.

"Trisha, what a fantastic dress! And I love your necklace."

"Thanks—"

"Cody, where've you been keeping yourself for the past
ten years?"

The conversation bubbled and swirled. Trisha managed
to make an occasional appropriate comment. When the
conversation drifted back to the inevitable "Remember
when—" theme, with happy reminiscences about events that
didn't include Trisha, Cody gave her a quick glance and then
pressed his thigh against hers under the table in a reassuring way.

The conversation also included many laughing refer-
ences to this afternoon's picnic. People felt foolish and
chagrined about their silly behavior, but the day was already taking on the stature of myth and legend. At reunions to come, this one would be remembered fondly,
reminisced over and endlessly rehashed just like all the other
memories that united these former classmates.

There was a brief program in which the reunion committee chairman thanked various people who had worked to put
the event together, and then the band started playing. Trisha
had never danced with Cody before, but there were no
awkward moments of adjusting to each other. They simply
fit together, their steps matching whether they were in each
other's arms or dancing apart to the music of one of the
hotter numbers popular when they were in high school.

He laughed as they gyrated to the beat. "I think I must have been more agile a decade ago."

Trisha just smiled. He looked agile enough. Oh, yes. Agile and sexy, handsome, virile, dynamic— She made herself stop before the list grew embarrassingly long.

"Do you go dancing often?" he asked when the music ended.

"Fairly often."

"May I ask with whom?"

She gave him the mysterious smile and tilt of the head that ten years ago she had practiced in front of a mirror, enjoying the flirty gesture even as she laughed at herself for using it. "Oh, with friends," she said with a deliberate, coquettish vagueness.

Once, to a dreamy slow tune, she felt a touch in her hair and tilted her head back to look up at him. "What are you doing?" They were dancing on the patio then, the lanterns casting romantic flickers over swaying bodies, the full moon silvering Cody's dark hair.

"Breathing in your hair."

She laughed. "Hair isn't something you can breathe."

"Oh, yes, it is. When it's hair like this." He nuzzled the pale golden cascade again, and his hand slid under her hair and caressed her back.

Later, there were finger sandwiches and coffee, a few more dances, a lineup for a class photo, and then the band was playing the old school song as a final number.

When the music ended, Candy tapped Cody on the shoulder. "Hey, a bunch of us are going out to Harrison's Pond," she whispered as if she didn't want everyone to hear. "How about you and Trisha coming along?"

Cody gave Trisha a questioning glance. "Interested?"

"What's going on at Harrison's Pond?" Trisha asked without committing herself. Ten years ago, Harrison's Pond, actually a small lake, had been a favorite partying and parking place. Trisha's only contact with it, however, had been daytime visits to toss dry bread scraps to the ducks that lived there.

"Oh, we'll build a fire," Candy said. "Drink a few beers. Go swimming in the moonlight. Just like old times."

"I'd have to go back to the motel to change clothes and pick up my swimsuit—"

"Who needs swimsuits?" Candy returned gaily with a flirty glance at Cody.

# Chapter Three

The reunion chairman grabbed the microphone again for a moment as everyone was leaving. "Don't forget the farewell breakfast at the Riverside Restaurant tomorrow morning. See you all then!"

Everyone milled toward the bottleneck of the main exit, but Cody took Trisha's hand and pulled her toward the open patio door. No one else was leaving that way.

"And now I know why," Cody groaned as they stepped into the freshly watered grass surrounding the patio.

Trisha's nylon-clad toes were immediately soaked, and her high heels sank into the soft ground, but Cody, never one to retreat or admit defeat, unexpectedly salvaged his choice of route. Before Trisha had time even to realize his intentions, she was in his arms, being carried across the wet grass and around the building to the sidewalk.

She would have been as astonished if a flying saucer had dropped out of the sky and whisked her away. Never once in her adult life had any man literally swept her off her feet and carried her as if she were some petite princess. She suddenly laughed for the sheer joy of it.

He stopped short. "Hey, what is this?" he grumbled. "A giggle instead of a swoon?"

"Sorry." She went into a "swoon," head flung back, eyes closed and arms drooping limply. "Is this better?"

"Much."

And it was over much too soon.

"So, do you want to go to Harrison's Pond?" Cody asked as he stood her upright on the sidewalk near the motorcycle.

"Do you?" she returned tentatively.

Cody's shoulders moved in an I-can-take-it-or-leave-it shrug, but then he tilted his head and looked at her thoughtfully. "You missed out on all that sort of thing in high school, didn't you?"

She nodded, moved by his unexpected perceptiveness.

"Then we'll do it," he said decisively. He grinned. "This is your life, Trisha Lassiter. A time trip into the past."

"For me, a revised past."

He took both her hands in his. "But a lot of what went on for some of us then wasn't really all that great. I can look back now and see that a lot of it was just damned stupid. Fortunately, I never got into drugs or even did much drinking, but I'd have been much better off if I'd spent more time studying and less time in general hell-raising and chasing around."

"You did have that little problem with speed," she agreed. And girls, she added to herself. Girls took up a lot of your time.

He smiled. "Would you believe I haven't had a speeding ticket for at least seven years?"

"Because you've stopped speeding? Or because you're better at evading capture?" Trisha teased tartly.

He feigned hurt. "You're looking at a man who has turned over a new leaf. Reformed. Changed his ways."

Trisha looked at him thoughtfully. *I'm looking at a man who is even more attractive than he was as a high school heartthrob, a man who is apparently still an expert at evading anything more than temporary capture.* But all she said was, "You'd rather not go out to Harrison's Pond, then?"

He lifted his hands and draped his forearms across her shoulders, his hands meeting under her tousled cascade of pale golden hair shimmering in the moonlight. The hard knuckles of his thumbs caressed the back of her neck, and his fingertips awakened her to a sensuous awareness of the the ridge of her spine.

"Whatever you want, I want, too."

The hint of intimacy in his tone and words brought a shivery prickle to Trisha's skin and reminded her of her earlier thought that there could be danger in a single evening with him.

She recklessly rejected the warning. "Let's go to the party."

The air was cooler now, and he wrapped his jacket around her for the motorcycle ride to her motel. He waited in the parking lot while she went in to change clothes. She removed her jewelry and shimmied out of the dress and damp-footed panty hose. She started to slip into jeans immediately but then changed her mind and put her swimsuit on first. No way was she going to be squirming around trying to change clothes in the bushes at the lake. And she definitely was *not* going skinny-dipping, no matter what anyone else might do.

She'd worn Cody's jacket up to her room, and she held it to her face for a moment, savoring the faint masculine scent of it, reluctant to give it up. But she could hardly keep it as a souvenir, she thought, smiling to herself. She slipped on a lightweight jacket of her own. She considered suggesting taking her car but decided against it. She wanted the full fantasy treatment she'd missed out on ten years ago: Harrison's Pond by moonlight, Cody Malone and a motorcycle.

They reversed the process at his motel, Trisha waiting outside while he went in to change. He returned in jeans and dark blue sweatshirt, rolled-up towel in his hand.

A fire already blazed within a circle of rocks by the time they arrived at Harrison's Pond. Trisha left her jacket on the motorcycle seat, anchoring it with the helmet. Blair and her husband arrived about the same time in their big, four-door sedan.

"I don't know what the hell got into her this afternoon with that ice-cube trick," Cody muttered.

"I guess you just have this devastating effect on women," Trisha teased.

"Present company included, I hope?" he teased back.

Cody held Trisha's hand as they approached the campfire. She recognized various people. Candy, of course, and her husband, Jerry. Brant Gordon, who'd joined up with the recently divorced Angela. Plus various other high school athletes and "Big Ten on Campus" types, the cream of the in crowd Trisha had never been a part of. Connie Melkin appeared to be alone.

"Drinks down in the water." Jerry waved a hand toward the small lake with moonlight flowing across it like a silvery pathway. A wooden raft floated in the center of the lake, the diving board almost touching the water because the old raft was half-waterlogged.

"Want something?" Cody asked Trisha.

"Whatever you're having."

"Hey, Cody!" somebody yelled as Cody knelt to fish the cans out of the water. "Remember the time that girl from Danville dared you to ride your bike across the pond?"

"And there was Cody," Candy said, "going glug-glug-glug as both he and the motorcycle slowly disappeared underwater."

Everyone laughed, Cody included, but he also wrinkled his nose at this reminder of another of his old misdeeds. For Trisha's benefit, he added an explanation. "They'd drained the lake to get rid of some unwanted fish and it was almost empty, but trying to ride my motorcycle across it still wasn't one of the smarter things I'd ever done. It took me a month to tear down the engine and get it running again after all the damage the water and mud did."

"But at least you weren't getting any speeding tickets during that time," Brant said, and everyone laughed again.

Trisha sat beside Cody, their backs against a log, their feet stretched toward the fire as the reminiscing continued. He draped his arm around her shoulders, and sometimes his fingers rubbed her upper arm gently, but she wasn't certain he was even aware he was doing that.

During a break in the conversation, Trisha whispered a suggestion to him. "How about a walk around the lake?"

She'd had her fill of listening to old stories, and he didn't seem much more interested in it than she was. She also remembered a spectacular view of Mount Shasta from the far side of the lake. The tall pines concealed it from this side.

"Sounds good."

"You two aren't leaving already, are you?" Candy asked when Trisha and Cody stood up.

"No, we're just going for a walk," Trisha said.

"Oh, a w-a-alk," Candy repeated, giggling and dragging the word out suggestively, and Trisha belatedly realized that to this crowd "going for a walk" hinted at something more exciting than an innocent stroll.

Trisha felt flustered, uncomfortably naive and inexperienced, just as she often had in high school. She wondered if Cody had also misinterpreted her "walk" suggestion.

"Okay, you guys, knock it off." Cody's tone was good-natured, but Trisha detected a small undercurrent of annoyance and a definite impression that he meant exactly what he said.

Trisha remembered where the trail was and led the way through the brushy willows and tall grass. Cody tucked his fingers into the waistband of her jeans as he followed along behind, as if he didn't want to let her out of his reach.

When they emerged from the willows, Cody brushed pine needles off a flat rock above the water. He sat down, pulling Trisha down beside him. Their feet dangled just a few inches above the dark surface. He scooted over to close the space between them, his thigh warm against hers. Trisha concentrated on the view of Mount Shasta, which was even more breathtaking than she remembered. It loomed with a timeless serenity, its snow-covered peak glowing with a soft radiance in the moonlight. A wisp of cloud clung to the top like a misty scarf trailing in the wind. A guffaw of laughter from across the lake made them both look in that direction.

"What did they talk about before there was all this reminiscing to do?" Trisha asked curiously.

Cody shook his head. "Damned if I can remember." He dismissed the old parties with a shrug. "Are you flying back to Hawaii immediately after the reunion?"

"I'm driving to San Francisco tomorrow and plan to spend a couple of days visiting galleries and shops there. I have plane reservations for Wednesday morning." She'd also decided not to wait until she got back to Kauai to call Dawn. The more she thought about it, the more uneasy she was that Dawn hadn't shown up at the reunion. Something could be wrong.

"How did you happen to move to Hawaii?"

"I just wanted to. . . get away."

"From what?"

She hesitated and then said honestly, "Me, I suppose."

"Did that work?"

"No. When you try to run away from yourself, there you are, tagging right along with you."

He smiled at her rather convoluted statement. "But something happened to make some big changes." He threaded his fingers through hers, and his hand felt warm and secure and masculine.

"I was in an accident. A kid on a skateboard crashed into me and knocked me into a concrete wall. I was in the hospital for several weeks with broken bones and a concussion, and then I was unable to do much of anything for a couple more months."

"That must have been rough. It also doesn't sound like an ideal situation for weight reduction and makeover," he observed.

"It wasn't. I wallowed in self-pity. . . and ate. I was mad at the world." She shook her head and laughed ruefully. "Everyone else was sailing along in the happy yacht of life, and I was trapped in the garbage scow. Then, when I thought things couldn't get any worse—"

"They got worse."

"Right. I wasn't driving my car, so, to save money, I dropped the insurance on it. And a hit-and-run driver rammed into it right there in the parking lot. Then my health insurance company tried to squirm out of paying some of my horrendous medical and home-nursing bills. By then I felt like the punching bag of the year. Fortunately, I had a lawyer who tackled my problems like a tiger going after raw meat. His name is Hugh and he worked a few miracles for me.''

Although Hugh had turned into much more than her lawyer; he was the best friend she'd ever had. They'd met before all her problems arose, but they really got to know each other during the legal battles. He was smart, tenacious and honest, a dedicated lawyer who took on a case because he believed in the rightness of it, not because of the size of the legal fee involved.

"Somehow I doubt a lawyer worked all the changes I see in you."

She nodded. That was true, of course. "But Hugh helped me see that even though I had no control over outside disasters in my life, I did have control over one aspect of it. My weight. No outside force had put those pounds on me, and no outside force was going to take them off. So I did it.''

It wasn't that simple, of course. After she'd recovered from the accident, it was still a two-year grind of careful nutrition, exercise and willpower before she got down to the weight she had maintained ever since. Plus dental work to straighten her teeth and a modeling class to work on her poise and posture. But, in spite of the truth in the statement that only she could *do* it, Hugh had been there every step of the way to help. He'd always seemed to know exactly what she needed, whether it was praise and encouragement or nagging and a stiff lecture.

But Hugh had done even more than help with her weight and self-image problems. She'd been working as a clerk at The Pink Turtle, just dabbling in jewelry design, and when the shop came up for sale, he'd encouraged her to buy it and get serious about her creative work. He'd also helped her find the financing to swing the deal.

Somewhere in there, he'd also started asking her to marry him, and briefly they had moved tentatively in that direction. But they'd stopped before they made the mistake of turning a great friendship into a mediocre marriage, and now, best buddies was what they were. She'd seen him through several romances, and she really hoped his current relationship would turn into the happy and lasting one he deserved. Especially because Nan seemed capable and levelheaded about money matters, and keeping track of money was not one of Hugh's strong points. More than once Trisha had helped him straighten out the financial jungle of his personal checking account.

"About this Hugh—" Cody began tentatively.

Suddenly, Trisha jumped to her feet. She hadn't come to Harrison's Pond for some big serious discussion, which was what this seemed to be turning into. She gave him a playful shove with her foot.

"I thought we came out here to party and swim!"

He caught her ankle, and for a moment she thought he was going to pursue the subject of Hugh, but then his thoughtful expression changed to a grin and his eyes gleamed with wicked mischief. Trisha tried to back away, suddenly uncertain what he had in mind, but his grip tightened on her ankle and his other hand reached for her waist.

"Oh, so it's swimming you want, is it?"

Then she knew. He was going to toss her fully clothed into the lake! She jerked her leg out of his grasp and whirled to make a dash for the trail, but she was barely off the rock before he tackled her around the knees. They went down together on the path, softened with a layer of old pine needles. She kicked and scrambled to get away, scrabbling along the ground with hands and elbows, but he came after her relentlessly, his body finally covering hers. She squirmed and twisted beneath him, but all she succeeded in doing was turning over on her back, and then she was helpless against his greater strength and weight. He held her captive with a knee on either side of her body and his hands pressing her shoulders down. Her chest rose and fell with the exertion of the tussle. Or perhaps it was something more than exertion that made her feel so breathless. . . .

He wasn't breathing as hard as she was, but his dark hair fell across his forehead. By then, they had wrestled off the trail and were only a few feet from the water. And suddenly she wasn't certain his intentions were as innocent as merely tossing her clothed into the lake.

"What are you going to do now?" she demanded warily.

"I'm trying to figure out how to get this T-shirt off you without getting my hand bitten." He looked perplexed, as if this were some complex problem in engineering.

"Get my T-shirt off!" she echoed in an outraged yelp.

She struggled again and got to a sitting position, but that was a mistake, because somehow he managed to yank the pink T-shirt off over her head. He grinned and waved it like a victory flag. She frantically grabbed for it, but he tossed it out of reach and pushed her back against the ground. Then he saw the white swimsuit she was wearing under the outer clothing.

"Ah, the cautious type." He grinned again, as if the swimsuit presented an interesting challenge but not an insurmountable problem. He scooted back against her bent knees and reached for the zipper on her jeans.

He had to release his grip on one shoulder to do that, and she clapped her free hand against the zipper. "Cody, what on earth are you *doing?*"

She was suddenly sharply aware that Cody was not like most of the safe, predictable men she dated. One of them might playfully push her into a swimming pool or purposely dance her into a dark corner for a stolen kiss, but it was always a gentlemanly sort of teasing. And there was nothing at all gentlemanly about the weld of Cody's body against her pelvis.

"You said you wanted to go swimming."

"Okay," she agreed cautiously. "Let's go swimming."

"And every woman deserves the memory of at least one wild skinny-dipping party at Harrison's Pond."

"Cody, I am *not* going skinny-dipping!"

"Aren't you?" he challenged. And while she was still protecting the zipper, he reached up and slipped the strap of the swimsuit off her shoulder. With a fingertip, he pushed it lower, his gaze suddenly riveted on the widening exposure of the full curve of her breast gleaming softly in the moonlight. She felt his gaze as if it were a hot caress on the bared skin.

Yet even with that distraction clogging her senses, Trisha saw a chance for escape. She twisted suddenly, throwing him sideways. But he didn't let go, and together they rolled like a many-legged ball down the slope of the shoreline. When the cold water hit Trisha's back, her shriek eclipsed any heard at the picnic that afternoon. Then they both splashed and floundered in the shallow but cold water. Trisha struggled to her knees but slipped and fell again. She realized why when her hand disappeared in the ooze beneath the water. There was a small detail she'd forgotten about Harrison's Pond. The bottom wasn't clean sand like the Hawaiian waters in which she usually swam; the bottom of Harrison's Pond was *mud*.

It roiled around them, squishy and gooey as some child's mud-pie recipe. She lifted a hand to brush wet hair out of her eyes and smeared the slick goo all over her face. She clenched her hand into a fist, and mud oozed between her fingers. She could even *taste* mud.

A yell came from across the small lake. "Hey, what's going on over there?"

"Trisha decided she wanted to go skinny-dipping!" Cody yelled back.

"I did not!"

"Ever thought about taking up mud wrestling?" he inquired, his grin audacious. Water dripped from his hair and glittered in his eyebrows, and mud bearded his chin, giving him the look of some devilishly handsome water demon. "I think you'd be quite good at it."

He scooted forward on the muddy bottom and rubbed a finger across her lips to brush away the mud. And then without warning, he leaned forward and kissed her.

He lifted his hands to cradle her face in what felt like a velvet cage, even though it was probably mud, and his mouth touched hers with sweet warmth. The warmth spread through her, and she forgot cold water and mud, forgot everything except the feel of his lips on hers. She was in warm sunlight, not cool moon glow; in a tropical lagoon, not a muddy pond. He scooted closer, circling her with his legs, and her arms rose to encircle his neck. His tongue tested the soft entrance to her mouth but didn't penetrate, and softly, tentatively, the tip of her own tongue met his. Finally, he took his lips away and studied her, not as if her hair clung wetly to her head or mud smeared her face but as if she was some newly discovered treasure.

"Are you glad you came to the reunion?" he whispered.

"I am."

"Glad you came?"

"Glad we both came."

Then, as if drawn by some newly created form of private gravity between them, he tilted his head and returned to her mouth.

Another yell. "Hey, you guys drown over there?"

Trisha heard the words only dimly, but some part of her echoed, *Yes, I'm drowning.* Drowning in the kiss, drowning in the feel of strong arms enveloping her, drowning in the special magic of Cody that was fully as tempting and tantalizing as it had been ten years ago.

He laughed softly when he finally raised his head. A blob of mud decorated the end of his nose. "What we need is a hot bath."

The way he put "we" and "hot bath" in the same sentence sent both hot thrill and cold panic jolting through Trisha. She scrambled to her feet.

"Race you to the raft!"

"Hey, no fair, you're already half undressed—"

"And whose doing is that?" she retorted.

She kicked her wet sandals toward the bank and tossed her jeans after them. Two strokes into the lake she glanced back and saw that he was still struggling to get out of the wet, heavy boots. Good Lord, she thought as he tore off the sweatshirt to reveal his bare chest, he *is* going to swim naked!

She turned her attention strictly to swimming then, briefly ducking underwater to remove the last traces of clinging mud, and then driving with long, steady strokes toward the raft. In spite of her head start, they reached the raft almost at the same time. She claimed victory, anyway. "Beat you!" she announced. Here in the center of the lake, with the muddy bottom some twelve or fifteen feet below, the water felt clean and fresh, cool silk against her skin.

He didn't argue with her claim. "Winner gets the prize, then."

"Which is?"

"Kiss from the loser, of course."

He wrapped his legs loosely around her, a muscular trap to keep her from escaping if she was so inclined, and she realized that he was in swim trunks after all. He'd put them on back at his motel room, just as she had her swimsuit. In spite of her relief, she couldn't help teasing him a bit. She snapped the elastic waistband of the swim trunks with a bold forefinger.

"Here I'd always thought you were this wild and crazy, skinny-dipping party animal. And now I find that you're just a shy, cautious—"

His legs tightened around her in a way that was neither shy nor cautious, and he cut off her words with the winner's kiss. His lips were also neither shy nor cautious, but they were already beginning to feel sweetly familiar. Maybe, she thought, because she'd kissed him so many times in youthful fantasy before the few times it actually happened, and then, afterward, relived the brief joy endlessly in painful memory. But neither fantasy nor memory could begin to compete with the powerful reality of kissing Cody in the flesh, and she gave herself up to the magic of it.

All her senses came alive to him and the moment. The warm taste of his mouth and the wet-male scent of him, the feel of their bodies tangled together beneath the surface and the drip of water from his hair on her nose. She heard his low murmur of approval, and then it deepened to a male growl of something stronger. Her eyes were closed and yet she could feel the glow of moonlight through her eyelids.

"Hey, are you guys really swimming out there?"

Trisha recognized Candy's voice this time. Her yell sounded suspicious. Trisha and Cody were on the far side of the raft where they couldn't be seen with only their heads out of the water.

Cody laughed softly. "Do you get the feeling we're not alone?"

To which Trisha's silent answer was, *And maybe it's a darn good thing we're not!*

"Cody?" Candy yelled.

"Sure, we're out here. The water's great," he called back.

Several splashes indicated swimming chaperons were on their way, so Trisha felt safe enough to do something uncharacteristically daring. She combed her fingers through the mat of hair on his chest, fulfillment of an old teenage fantasy, and swirled a silky strand around her fingertip. In the moonlight she saw a surprised lift of Cody's eyebrows.

"Well, well," he said with a meaningful inflection.

Her hand instantly retreated to flutter in the water, as if she'd only accidentally encountered his chest while paddling. "Well, well, what?" she returned defensively.

He grinned. "Nothing. Just, well, well."

Two swimmers arrived then. Trisha hoisted herself up on the raft and Cody followed. With four people on it, the old raft sank even lower. Several more swimmers were on their way, but most of the party group was just standing around the campfire watching. Candy, decorously covered with a swimsuit in spite of her flirtatious talk, was still standing at the edge of the pond dipping a toe in the water.

"Hey, I think this water's about forty degrees colder than it used to be!" she called.

"No, it isn't," her husband yelled back from the raft. "It's just that we were all about forty degrees hotter back then."

Candy finally made it out to the raft. The men were horsing around, knocking each other off the raft in an overage, king-of-the-mountain game. Trisha helped Candy get on the raft. In spite of her weight complaints, her ample figure looked voluptuously attractive in the one-piece bathing suit.

"I am freezing my buns off," Candy grumbled. She wrapped her arms around herself. "I recall this being a lot more fun ten years ago."

*I wouldn't know,* Trisha thought tartly. *I wasn't invited.* But at the moment, she had to admit that she, too, was definitely getting chilled. Out of the protective covering of water, the night air felt distinctly cold against bare, wet skin.

Cody's head and shoulders suddenly appeared next to her goose-bumped legs. He touched her thigh with his palm. "You're getting cold. Let's go." It was more command than suggestion, but she didn't argue. The water felt almost warm when she slipped back into it.

All Cody's clothes were soaked, and Trisha's jeans were stiff and clammy, but she did have a dry T-shirt. Trying to get into the wet denim jeans reminded her of those awful days when she'd buy something a size too small, vowing to lose weight to fit into it, only to find that she didn't lose the weight and undersize pants bore a painful resemblance to a full-length tourniquet.

Back at the campfire, Cody draped his wet sweatshirt over a couple of sticks of wood to dry. Both he and Trisha stood close to the fire, turning every minute or two to try to dry both the front and rear of their jeans. Blair and her husband left, then several more couples, including Candy and Jerry.

"We're running up a baby-sitting bill like you wouldn't believe," Candy said, sighing. "But we'll see you all at breakfast in the morning. Now don't you guys do anything out here that we wouldn't do. Especially you, Cody." She waggled a finger at him.

Within a few minutes, only Trisha, Cody, Angela and Brant remained at the fire.

"I vote for making it an all-night party," Brant said. He draped an arm around Angela. "We can go to the breakfast right from here."

"Actually, I think it's about time we took off, don't you?" Cody looked at Trisha.

"Hey, c'mon, don't be party poopers. You don't have to go anywhere, do you, Angela?" Brant asked.

"I really should. Mike has the kids this weekend, but sometimes they wake up in the middle of the night and want to call and talk to me." Mike Winters, Angela's ex, hadn't shown up at the picnic or dance. Apparently, Angela had gotten custody of the class reunion. "They're confused and upset by the divorce." Words which emphasized that, in spite of being out here acting like carefree teenagers, they all had adult problems and responsibilities.

Trisha offered no opinion on ending the party. It had suddenly occurred to her that she would soon have to deal with a rather awkward moment. She and Cody were no longer kids, and this was no study date.

Cody helped put out the campfire, and then Trisha climbed on the motorcycle behind him for the ride back to town. At the motel, Cody parked the motorcycle directly beneath the second-story door to her room. She stalled for time by making a little ceremony out of removing her helmet and tucking it in the luggage box.

"You don't need to walk me to the door," she suggested. She smiled brightly. "Thanks for a wonderful time—"

He draped an arm lightly around her shoulders. "I may have had many a teenage fault, but not walking the girl I was with to the door wasn't one of them."

At the door, she stuck the key in the lock and then turned to face him under the amber glow of the coach lights lining the balcony. Here it was, that awkward moment. She could think of nothing but a repetition of what she'd already said.

"Thanks again. I had a marvelous time—"

He lifted one arm and braced his hand against the door-jamb, creating a pocket of intimacy around them. He tilted his head. "Really?"

In the wet, smoke-scented clothes, Trisha felt rather like a wiener that had tried to barbecue itself inside a soggy bun, but, yes, she'd had fun. Although she suspected that the re-run of a teenage party rite had nothing to do with it. It was Cody. And she could feel herself falling under his spell just as if she were still a breathless teenager. His laugh, his dark good looks, his powerful masculinity, his kisses. Oh yes, his kisses....

But all she could say, brightly if a bit inanely was, "Yes, really."

His free hand lifted to her throat, his fingers curving around the back of her neck. "Do you have to leave tomorrow? I was thinking that after we went to the reunion breakfast, we could spend the day together. Just the two of us, without food fights or mud baths or a clutter of adolescent memories."

His fingertips lightly massaged her nape and then slid upward through her hair, a caress that sent a tingle careering through her that was all out of proportion to the intensity of the light touch.

She swallowed and floundered for an answer. Intimate...unacceptable!...possibilities for the day flooded her mind. Finally, she detoured a direct answer by responding with a cautious question. "What did you have in mind?"

"I'm kind of an antique-car buff, and there's a car show down at Redding tomorrow. Or if that doesn't interest you, maybe a boat ride on Shasta Lake?"

The propriety of the suggestions relieved her, and she considered the plans she'd already made to leave the next day so she could spend two days in San Francisco before flying home. The plans weren't chiseled in stone, however. She could wait until Monday to drive to San Francisco, although that would mean she'd have only one day to visit the galleries and shops.

*Which is plenty!* an eager inner voice assured her.

But going to the reunion breakfast and then spending the entire day with Cody would be stretching the "punctuation mark" symbolism beyond all reasonable limits....

So she gave her answer for the simple reason that it was what she really wanted to do. "I'd love to stay and go to the car show." Not adding the most important part. *With you.*

"Good. I had fun tonight, too, Trisha."

"Did you really intend to...make me go skinny-dipping?"

He smiled. "I guess you'll just have to wonder about that. But I do intend to do this."

His hand cradled her chin and his mouth dipped to hers. The kiss was light, not platonic but almost chaste, as if he intended it merely as a quick good-night gesture. Gentle pressure of lips, no invasion of tongue, no contact of bodies. She lifted one hand and clasped his wrist. When he lifted his head, his face was in shadows, hers lifted to the amber light. His thumb stroked the corner of her mouth, and his conversational tone went rough as he said, "But, what I really want to do is *this.*"

His arms encircled her, one slipping down to mold the pliable length of her body against his, the other finding bare skin under her T-shirt, where the back of her still-damp swimsuit dipped below her waist. She closed her eyes as she lifted her arms to encircle his neck and turned her face up to meet his.

His tongue flicked with tantalizing sweetness across her lower lip and then plunged inside. She didn't retreat from the hungry passion. Some little voice told her she should, but she ignored it. She savored the strength and passion of the kiss and returned it. She felt as if the heat of him were pouring into her, as if she were an empty glass filling with a sweet and heady wine. She drank it in, her fingertips on his neck and in his hair, echoing the caress of his hand roaming her back with a tantalizing combination of kitten tenderness and masculine roughness. A strong fingertip traced the lower curve of the swimsuit, dipping inside just far enough to send a sweet shiver dancing through her. She felt the awakening of desires that went far beyond her innocent teenage fantasies of long ago.

But just as his hand moved around to the curve of her breast, the door to the next room whipped open.

"Are you two going to stand around and talk all night?" asked a rumpled-looking middle-aged man in the bottom half of striped pajamas.

In embarrassment, Trisha gushed an elaborate apology, even though it didn't seem to her that they'd been noisy at all. For the last few moments, in fact, there had been silence between them. "We're so sorry! We didn't realize we were disturbing you—"

"Ask him in or kick him out. Makes no difference to me," the man grumbled. "Just *do* it."

The door slammed.

Trisha swallowed. Uncomfortably she said, "Well, that was a . . . uh . . . surprise."

Cody laughed. "Perhaps not quite as effective as a cold shower but certainly a close second. Somehow I don't think I'm going to be invited in." He sounded teasing rather than angry or annoyed, however.

His observation was also quite true. She was still breathless from the kiss, but the brief, dangerous moment of susceptibility was behind her.

"Did you expect to be?" she challenged lightly.

He tilted his head. "No. Not really." He didn't say the words but there was something in his slow smile that added, *Not yet, anyway.* "So I'll see you in the morning, then. About eight-thirty?"

"Fine. I'm looking forward to it."

He kissed her again, but this time it was just a friendly peck on the cheek. Although her cheek did carry the brand of the kiss in the form of a small but potent hot spot for a disproportionate length of time.

# *Chapter Four*

The breakfast at the restaurant overlooking the river was buffet-style. With the rattle of trays and silverware, the hum of conversation and an occasional outburst of laughter, it was a noisy, cheerful place. Trisha and Cody filled their trays with juice, ham and scrambled eggs, muffins and coffee. She wore a pale blue jumpsuit and Cody was in casual slacks. She could see the speculation as people waved and called greetings. They were wondering if she and Cody had spent the night together, of course.

And she, exchanging an amused glance with Cody, was inclined to let them wonder.

She wasn't particularly eager to sit through more reminiscing with the group who'd been at Harrison's Pond, so she wasn't sorry when Cody led the way to empty chairs at the end of one of the long tables that had been set up for the reunion crowd. Unexpectedly, the seat next to Cody was taken by Mr. Longview, who had been football coach at the high school ten years ago but was now retired. Trisha knew that a number of their old teachers had been invited to the reunion events, although only a few were attending.

Cody and his former coach talked about some of the more memorable games of that era, and then Mr. Longview said,

"I hear you're now in the scientific field...a volcanologist?" He sounded, if not skeptical, at least a bit tentative about the accuracy of the statement.

"That's right. I'm presently working up at Mount St. Helens. Although there isn't much going on there right now."

Mount St. Helens, which was located not far from the city in southwestern Washington where Cody lived, had erupted violently in 1980 after being inactive for over a hundred years. Trisha and her parents were living in a small town in the eastern part of Washington State at the time, and she well remembered the several inches of gritty ash that had blanketed their house.

"I must say I'm surprised," Mr. Longview admitted.

Cody laughed. "I guess it looked as if I were, as the old saying goes, headed for hell in a hand basket when I was in high school."

Mr. Longview's smile acknowledged as much. "How did you happen to get into this line of work?" he asked, a question about which Trisha was also curious.

"I suppose I...borrowed it from my younger brother. He was always interested in the prehistoric era, anything from cavemen to dinosaurs, and volcanoes also seem to have a connection with a prehistoric past."

The unexpectedly somber way in which Cody spoke of his younger brother stopped Trisha's forkful of scrambled eggs halfway to her mouth. He'd used the past tense, and she saw the harsh tightening of his mouth and felt the jerk of his leg under the table. She hadn't had any classes with David Malone, who was a year or so younger than Cody, but she remembered him as nice looking and quiet, neither the athlete or hell-raiser that Cody had been. Had something happened to David?

Mr. Longview answered that question when he said quietly, "I remember the accident. It was a terrible tragedy."

Cody nodded, his face uncharacteristically grim, and for a moment an invisible shell seemed to enclose him. His brother was dead, Trisha realized in shock.

"Cody, I didn't know. I'm so sorry—"

Beneath the table she squeezed his thigh with her hand, not realizing until she'd done it that the impulsive gesture of sympathy was too intimate. But he just gave her a grateful glance and moved his leg over closer to hers. Then he took a sip of coffee and his expression changed, as if he'd determinedly put the unhappy thoughts behind him. His voice was in its normal cheerful range when he spoke, and the grim moment passed.

"I had a little trouble getting into college, because my grades were not great." He smiled ruefully at the understatement. "But when I made it in, I went year-round to get through faster. I got my degree in geology from the University of California at Davis, and I've worked around several active volcanoes since then. Pinatubo in the Philippines was one of the most exciting."

"An interesting, if risky, choice of occupation," Mr. Longview observed. "I remember seeing in the news about the Pinatubo eruption. And then there was that big one down in Colombia that caught several scientists off guard."

Cody nodded. "The Galeras volcano. Even with all the modern technology that's available, a lot of work remains to be done in the area of accurate prediction of volcanic eruptions. I'm very interested in that. I'm also planning to start work on my doctorate one of these days. Eventually I'd like to teach on the university level."

Cody, the eager student—and teacher? *Dr.* Cody Malone? That was indeed a change from the teenage boy who'd romanced her in order to get out of doing an English paper himself. Cody glanced at her and apparently recognized her thoughts.

He smiled. "Who'd of thunk it?" he whispered in a truthful, if ungrammatical, observation.

The reunion chairman made another little speech, and then the gathering began to break up. Trisha was glad she'd come but also not sorry this official part of the event was over. She felt as if she were holding a delicious and very private secret, the knowledge that she and Cody still had the rest of the day together while everyone else went their separate ways. Everyone seemed to want to say something in parting to him, with Trisha included because he kept a tight hold on her hand, and she found herself saying bright goodbyes and, "Be sure to look me up if you ever get to Kauai," to lots of people.

Finally, they escaped to the motorcycle parked at the curb outside.

"Intcresting, but every ten years is often enough for that, as far as I'm concerned," Cody said as he handed her a helmet. "I'm more interested in the future than the good ol' days."

Which was exactly how Trisha felt.

He again raised the question of using a different form of transportation, but Trisha shook her head. It was a gloriously sunny morning, and riding the motorcycle, with no connection to her long-ago fantasies or yesterday's "punctuation mark" excuse for being with him, was exactly what she wanted. Maybe because it gave her a wonderful reason to wrap her arms around him on the ride to the car show in Redding.

The show was a big one, several hundred vehicles gleaming in the California sunshine. There was everything from a wonderful old 1909 Oakland, a make Trisha had never even heard of, to Mustangs and Thunderbirds from the early seventies. A salesman hawked a special car polish, and music blared raucously from a loudspeaker. Most of the music was from the fifties, with an occasional excursion into something older. When a jazzy rendition of, "Yes, Sir, That's My Baby" played, a trio of flapper-costumed dancers did an energetic Charleston on a small wooden stage. Squeals from the rides at a carnival set up across the street added to the holiday atmosphere.

Trisha felt wonderfully happy and lighthearted. She remembered a silly knock-knock joke to tell Cody, and he had another light-bulb one for her. He also amused her with a story about a tourist who'd come to Mount St. Helens and complained because there was no elevator to provide her with a view from the top.

"We have our Hawaiian volcanoes, too. Kilauea over on the Big Island has been active rather frequently for several years now," she reminded him. She laughed. "But I don't think it has an elevator, either."

The cars were divided by decades into rows, and Trisha and Cody strolled through the fifties row twice because Cody said those were his favorites. He paused to admire a '57 Chevy, flamboyant with oversize tail fins and glittery with chrome.

"I restored one like that last year, working on it in my spare time." He gave her a speculative glance. "What do you do in your spare time?"

"I don't have much of it," she admitted. "The Pink Turtle and my jewelry designing keep me very busy. But I do like to surf and swim, and there are some wonderful hiking trails on the island."

"I've never been to Hawaii. If I showed up on your doorstep, maybe we could go hiking and surfing...and dancing?"

The possibility made Trisha's heart dance to a wild drumbeat that was out of tempo with Elvis's rendition of "Love Me Tender" coming from the loudspeaker, but she managed to say lightly, "That could probably be arranged." Then, wanting him to know she really meant it, she added more seriously, "If you ever do get to Hawaii, to visit the volcano or for any other reason, I really do hope you'll look me up."

She hadn't been *insincere* in inviting other old classmates to visit her if they ever got to Kauai, but Cody was the only one who she really hoped would accept.

Cody kept her hand in his except when they were filling out sheets to vote for their favorite cars, good-naturedly disagreeing on a couple. After stuffing their ballots in the cardboard box, they wandered through a flea market set up on the far side of the grounds. Strange objects were for sale: hats made of yarn knit around soft-drink cans, earrings that had the head end of a pig on one earring, the rear end on the other, used jeans, old car parts. They walked with arms around each other's waists and laughed at everything...and nothing. Cody bought her a teddy bear—"He looks so sad I can't just leave him there," Cody said—and she laughingly bought him a key chain decorated with an outrageous hula girl. They ate hotdogs and drank soft drinks, topping it all off with cotton candy. Trisha allowed herself such a dietary extravagance a couple of times a year, and this was surely a day on which to spend that allowance.

A couple of times she considered asking about his brother David's death and how it had happened, but it didn't seem the right time to remind him of what she knew had been a painful experience.

After the flea market, they went to the carnival. They threw dimes at containers that almost seemed to lean to avoid catching the coins. They rode a whirling monstrosity called Screamin' Lena, after which she had to lean against him to regain her equilibrium. They went through the comic-scary House of Mystery and wound up with a ride on the old-fashioned Ferris wheel. At the top of the third revolution, Cody kissed her, holding warm lips to hers all the way around the circle until they were at the top again.

And it wasn't their height in the sky that made her feel as if she were floating on the very top of the world.

It wasn't until they were headed back to Horton on the motorcycle that she thudded back to earth. Wonderful as it had been, the reunion was definitely over now. Tomorrow she would drive to San Francisco and Cody would head in the opposite direction to Vancouver. After that, an ocean would separate them.

But between now and then lay tonight.... A night that she suspected she didn't have to spend alone if she didn't want to.

She instantly rejected that tantalizing thought. When they got to the motel she'd just thank him again for a wonderful time and say goodbye.

In the parking lot of the motel, she climbed off the motorcycle first. She removed her helmet and placed it in the luggage box. Who, she wondered with a certain pang, usually wore that extra helmet? She pushed that thought aside. Irrelevant.

"It's been a wonderful day, Cody. A wonderful reunion. Thank you so much—"

He scowled lightly. "That sounds like goodbye."

"Well—"

"Oh, no. You're not getting rid of me that easily." He glanced at his watch. "I'll pick you up at seven-thirty and we'll have dinner together."

Trisha swallowed. "And—then?"

He tilted his head, his slow and lazy smile just like those that had revved her heartbeat ten years ago. And still did.

"And then, we'll see." The kiss he planted on her lips was quick. But not lacking in sweet promise.

In the motel room she set the teddy bear on the dresser where she could see him, and smiled at his sad expression. She slipped out of the blue jumpsuit, started to put it on a hanger but folded and placed it in the suitcase, instead. She should get everything packed tonight so she'd be ready to leave early in the morning.

She showered, and in panties and bra stood in front of the open closet looking at the remaining clothes she'd brought with her. The strawberry, halter-topped sundress with matching jacket would be suitable for dinner—

Unexpectedly, she shivered lightly. Because she had the air conditioner turned up too high?

No.

Because she had a sudden vision of Cody removing that jacket. Removing it right here in this room, his eyes holding hers as he slid it from her shoulders with sensuous slowness. A kiss on her throat, his hands slipping around her body to slide the zipper of her sundress down. And she eagerly returning the intimate gesture, unbuttoning his shirt, running her hands through the dark mat of his chest hair....

She was no longer cold. Beads of perspiration gathered and formed a trickle between her breasts.

She knew what she should do. Call and tell him she'd decided to grab a sandwich at the coffee shop and turn in early so she could get an early start tomorrow.

That idea brought instant rebellion. She *wanted* to have dinner with him.

Surely there was no harm in that, she rationalized. She was, after all, a woman with willpower and a definite code to guide her. It would be rude *not* to accept, after how nice he'd been to her. They'd just have a pleasant dinner, share more laughter and talk, thank each other for the good times and say goodbye.

*So how many other fairy tales do you know?* her little inner voice snapped with uncharacteristic cynicism.

She dropped to the bed, hands clamped between her knees, suddenly aware that the simple, carefree day had taken on complications. She had blithely stepped into something far more intense and powerful than she had anticipated, perhaps more powerful than she was prepared to handle.

Because she was still attracted to Cody, attracted to him as a mature woman, not a teenager with romantic fantasies. Where there had once been dreamy crush, adult emotions and desires now surged. If she went to dinner with him, she knew what would happen afterward. Look how easily his dinner invitation had melted through her decision to say goodbye as soon as they returned to the motel.

*So why not let it happen?*

What had happened between her and Cody ten years ago no longer felt like a wound that had healed on the surface but left a sore spot underneath. She knew that Cody sincerely regretted what he had done back then. He had also changed and matured. He'd tamed his flirtation with speed. He'd dropped his irresponsible attitude toward studies and worked hard to become a volcanologist.

The night's possibilities shimmered like a jewel glittering in moonlight. A jewel that she had only to reach out and snatch.

Yet if she recklessly grabbed it, what then? Cody may have matured and changed in many ways, but none of that meant he'd reformed in matters of the heart, and she was still far more vulnerable to heartbreak than he was. The possibility of his someday visiting Hawaii was no more substantial than the seafoam washing up on her island; only tonight was a concrete reality.

She'd had her Cinderella night of magic at the ball. She'd experienced a party at Harrison's Pond, complete with requisite dunking. She'd had a wonderful day with Cody.

Time to quit while she was ahead, before she got in too deep both emotionally and physically.

In a sudden rush to escape before her resolve weakened, she haphazardly stuffed her things into the suitcase, taking care only with the borrowed red dress. The jeans and swimsuit from last night's party at Harrison's Pond were still damp, and she found a plastic bag for them. She scooped her makeup into the cosmetics case and slipped into the comfortable jumpsuit again. In fifteen minutes she was packed and ready to go.

She'd paid in advance, so she didn't have to stop at the office. She placed the room key on the nightstand and made a final tour of the room to be sure she hadn't left anything. She had the door half-open before she stopped short.

She couldn't just walk out without saying a word to Cody. That kind of rudeness just wasn't part of her character. Yet if she talked to him, she had the uneasy feeling all her firm resolve would turn as insubstantial as the cotton candy she'd shared with him.

She opened the phone book and ran a fingernail down the list of motel names until she came to the one where Cody was staying. She dialed the number.

"Good evening, Lone Pine Motel."

"I'd like to leave a message for Mr. Malone in room twenty-nine, please." She'd noted the room number when she waited at the motorcycle while he changed clothes after the dance yesterday night.

"You can dial him direct—"

"No, I... prefer to leave a message. Please just tell him that Miss Lassiter won't be able to have dinner with him, after all. And please tell him thanks for everything."

The woman repeated the message in a bored tone.

"Yes, that's it. Thank you. And I'd appreciate it if you'd see that he gets the message within the next half hour."

She picked up her suitcase and cosmetics case and set them outside the door. And again she paused, her hand on the knob. Once she closed that door behind her, everything would be over, the conclusive ending on the second and final installment of her roller-coaster involvement with Cody Malone.

Decisively she closed the door.

* * *

She drove for several hours, determinedly thinking about
The Pink Turtle, her roommate Leslie's upcoming wedding, anything but Cody. She stopped once to have a light
dinner of soup and salad, and when she got sleepy, she
turned off the freeway and rented a motel room.

Unfortunately, as soon as she was in bed, sleep felt as far
away as the next reunion. Which she'd already decided she
didn't plan to attend. Images of Cody flitted through her
mind like the pages of some personal pinup calendar. Cody
in his charcoal-colored suit at the dance...Cody stripping
off his sweatshirt at the lake...Cody's face in close-up just
before he kissed her. And there were more meaningful images, too. Cody laughing, obviously enjoying being with
her. Cody momentarily somber when he thought about his
brother. Cody saying he might appear on her doorstep....

With the same determination she had once used to switch
her thoughts to carrot sticks when the image of a fudge
sundae attacked her, she switched her sleepless thoughts to
Dawn. She turned on the bedside lamp and checked her
watch, thinking she might call Dawn now, but, with the time
difference between California and Minnesota, she decided
it was too late for that. So she wound up watching a late-
night movie that fortunately was dull enough to put her to
sleep.

She drove the remaining distance to San Francisco the
following morning and spent the afternoon visiting several
of the galleries on her to-see list. She tried to call Dawn that
evening but got no answer.

The following evening, she decided to give Dawn's number one more try. This time, a voice still familiar even after
ten years answered.

"Hi, Dawn. This is Trisha."

"Trisha? *Trisha?* I can't believe it! I thought you'd fallen
off the end of the earth somewhere!"

"No, just Hawaii."

Meeting in person would have been better, but they had
a wonderful phone reunion. Nothing disastrous had kept
Dawn from the class reunion. She said the reason she hadn't

attended was that only a few days after sending in her reunion fee she'd learned she was pregnant.

"The doctor said it would be okay if I went, but after trying for all these years to get pregnant, I decided I just wasn't going to take any chances traveling."

"Dawn, that's wonderful! I'm so happy for you."

They talked about everything. The coming baby and Dawn and her husband's moves around the country as he climbed the corporate ladder. How the reunion committee had located Trisha by following addresses through several of her parents' moves. Trisha's weight loss and The Pink Turtle. Dawn wanted to know all about their former classmates, "especially the really catty stuff" as she laughingly put it.

Trisha related everything she'd seen and all the gossip she'd picked up here and there, trying not to be *too* catty in the process.

"What about that guy you had the big crush on?" It took Dawn a moment to dredge up the name. "Cody Malone. The *gorgeous* Cody Malone."

"Yes, he was there. He's been to college and is now a volcanologist working up at Mount St. Helens. He looks as good as ever, and still has women falling all over him. Actually, he...gave me quite a rush."

"Really? Trisha, tell me all!"

Trisha told all.

"So, are you going to see him again? He sounds like the kind of guy who just might do something romantic like jump on a plane and fly over to Hawaii to see you!"

"I doubt that." Trying to make an amusing story of what she'd done, Trisha related the less-than-romantic ending of her reunion relationship with Cody. To her surprise, Dawn's reaction was mild disapproval.

"Don't you think you may have treated him a little unfairly? I always thought he might be a pretty special guy if he ever got beyond that teenage-jock, heartthrob-of-Horton-High mind-set. And it sounds as if he has."

Trisha didn't object to the hint of criticism. She and Dawn had always been able to be honest with each other. But her tone was a little indignant when she said, "You mean you think I should have leapt into bed with him, just like that?"

"No, of course not. But you didn't need to stand him up."

"Oh, come on. What if I'd gone to the reunion looking just as I did ten years ago? He probably wouldn't have looked twice at me. Who needs a guy like that?"

"What if he'd returned with a potbelly, chewing a toothpick and wearing a polyester plaid leisure suit? Would you have looked twice at *him?*"

That unlikely vision of Cody made Trisha laugh, but then she considered the question seriously. How would she have felt about Cody if he weren't just as attractive... no, even *more* attractive...than he'd been ten years ago? The old line about not throwing stones if you're standing in a glass house came to mind.

"Look, what-ifs are irrelevant," Dawn said firmly. "You're both what you are right now, and what matters is that you're attracted to him, and the feeling is apparently mutual."

"So what are you suggesting?"

"Go for it. Call him up. Admit you panicked but you're sorry and you'd really like to see or hear from him again."

"I don't have his phone number."

Dawn gave an exaggerated sigh. "You're acting like the old Trisha again. I thought this was the new-and-improved model. Surely you've heard of a service called 'Information'?"

Trisha started to protest that Cody might have an unlisted number. Otherwise, he'd probably have women calling at all hours of the day and night. But then she guiltily realized that Dawn was right. She was acting exactly like the old Trisha who tended to run and hide, if not in a corner or behind the nearest tree, at least behind the nearest excuse for avoiding challenge or an uncomfortable situation.

She didn't commit herself, but she did say, "Okay, I'll think about it."

They talked a while longer, promising to write and never lose contact again.

"Send a photo," Dawn added.

"And you take care of yourself and that baby," Trisha concluded.

Trisha felt good after the phone call, warmed by the contact with her old friend. She watched TV for a while, but she couldn't keep her mind on the problems in the situation comedy. What Dawn had said kept churning around in her head.

Maybe she had overreacted. She'd thought of her leaving Horton without seeing Cody again as a protective action of self-survival, but maybe it was simply that the old insecure Trisha had surfaced. And panicked and run.

They'd had such a wonderful time. Laughed and danced, swam and kissed. He'd seemed genuinely interested in her as a person, not just a one-night stand to enliven a reunion weekend. Visions of him swam through her head like genies released from a bottle.

She had a shaky awareness of just how easily her heart could become deeply involved with Cody, and the possible dangers involved, but she recklessly rejected the warning.

She was going to call him. Now.

# Chapter Five

Long-distance information service readily supplied a telephone number for Cody Malone in Vancouver, Washington. Using her credit card, she briskly made the call. Yet her finger slid toward the disconnect button as the phone rang on the other end of the line. Perhaps she should think this through a little more thoroughly....

"Hello."

The voice momentarily froze Trisha's finger motionless and stunned her into silence. It had never occurred to her that a woman might answer Cody's phone.

Now don't get in a big stew over nothing, she told herself hastily. Wrong numbers happen. She forced herself to say with polite formality, "Is this the Cody Malone residence in Vancouver, Washington?"

"Yes, it is." A cheerful-sounding voice, young and attractive.

Not a wrong number. Okay, there were other reasonable possibilities. A sister? No. Cody's mother had been dead for a long time, and there'd been only Cody, his younger brother David and their father living in the little house in Horton that was bachelor messy the only time Trisha had seen inside it. So, secretary or housekeeper working at his apartment? Possibly. She glanced at her watch. But not a *likely* possibility at eight-thirty in the evening.

She decided to stop speculating. Her next question certainly fractured the rules of polite telephone etiquette, but she bluntly asked it anyway. "Who is this?"

"This is Melissa. Cody's not home yet, but he should be back soon. May I take a message?"

Melissa sounded comfortable, confident and very much at home. Perhaps a bit curious about the caller's identity, but too secure to be alarmed. In the background, Trisha could hear the sound of television laughter and chatter, as if Cody and the woman had been spending a companionable evening at home together. Then another unidentifiable noise shrilled over the line.

"Oh, there's the buzzer on my cookies," Melissa said. "Hold on a minute, will you, while I take them out of the oven."

Trisha had questioned Cody about whether he was married; obviously, she should have asked a few more questions about current intimate relationships and living arrangements.

She was half inclined to inform trusting Melissa what her guy had been up to at his class reunion, but she didn't. She just hung up before the woman returned.

He'd done it to her again, Trisha thought unhappily. Zapped her like an insect in a cloud of bug spray.

Pain and disappointment washed through her, an echo of the hurt of ten years ago. Her mouth felt dry and sour, her throat tight. Yet she wasn't that same insecure, vulnerable girl she reminded herself firmly. She'd found the mature Cody wildly attractive, but her feelings for him weren't like the devastating crush that had once tied her in knots.

And she wasn't sorry she'd tried to call him. If she hadn't, she'd always have thought she'd treated him unfairly, or wondered if she'd let the resurfacing of old insecurities destroy the possibility of a new relationship.

Now she knew. Cody Malone was still doing his magic juggling act, keeping several women spinning in the air at once, just as he had when he was the reigning heartthrob of Horton High.

And Trisha had no intention of joining the act.

The apartment was empty when Trisha unlocked the front door. She stopped in the doorway, startled at just how empty it was, momentarily wondering if they'd been wiped out by a furniture burglar. But then she realized that it was nothing that dramatic. The living room furniture belonged to Leslie, and she had no doubt just moved it over to her fiancé's apartment. Leslie and Tyler were starting marriage on a very slender shoestring, with some very old furniture. But lots of love. Which Trisha had to admit she sometimes envied.

She glanced at her watch. Leslie was still at the doctor's office where she worked as receptionist, of course. After the long flight from San Francisco to Honolulu, then another hop over to Kauai, Trisha felt as if it should be time for bed. But with the time difference between Hawaii and the mainland, it was still only late afternoon.

She dropped her suitcase and cosmetics case on the floor in her bedroom, glad to be home. Her appreciative gaze took in the familiar handmade quilt on her bed, a treasure she'd bought from an elderly island woman whose work Trisha now proudly displayed in her shop. The shell lamp she'd made herself, a calendar of colorful sea creatures given to her by Hugh, a Hawaiian seascape done by one of the popular artists whose works she also displayed in her shop. The clutter on the corner table where she did her jewelry making was just as she'd left it, and Leslie had put a welcome-home vase of fresh flowers on the nightstand.

She was going to miss sweet and lively Leslie, who would be her roommate only until the wedding this coming Saturday evening. But she had to admit that having the extra space after Leslie moved out would be nice. At one time, she couldn't afford the apartment alone, but The Pink Turtle was doing so well now that she'd decided not to look for another roommate to share expenses. She planned to turn the bedroom Leslie now occupied into a jewelry-making workshop that would be much more spacious and comfortable than the cramped corner of her bedroom.

She threw open a window, letting in the sweet fragrance of the creamy plumeria growing just outside her bedroom. Across the lane, a row of tulip trees flamed with blooms of fiery red streaked with yellow. Clouds swathed the top of Mount Waialeale, often called the wettest place on earth, but here the sky was fairy-tale blue and the air balmy. The apartment was too far from the ocean to offer the sound of surf, but she knew it was out there, sometimes mild, sometimes wild.

Yes, it was great to be home.

She unpacked, taking special care with the borrowed red dress, and dropping things to take to the laundry into a pile on the floor. She wrinkled her nose when she came to the plastic bag of jeans and swimsuit that were still slightly damp, traces of Harrison's Pond mud also still clinging to the jeans.

When she was through putting everything away, she had one item remaining. The sad-looking teddy bear that Cody had bought for her. For a moment, her fingertips lingered on the fuzzy face...and Cody's image lingered in her mind. She'd kept him out of her surface thoughts on the flight home, although she'd been aware of him stomping around in the subterranean depths of her mind, ready to raise havoc if she'd let him. Now she decisively stuffed the teddy bear into a box on the closet shelf and Cody into a mental box and closed the door on both of them.

She called The Pink Turtle, which she had left in the competent hands of her full-time clerk, Anne McGiven. Everything was fine there, except that Mrs. Okamoto had brought in two lovely new quilts, and Anne hadn't found any space to display them. Trisha would be so glad when the new and larger space was ready for occupancy.

With that thought in mind, she decided to call Hugh and ask how work on the building was coming, but before she could dial, the phone rang. It was her roommate, calling from the office.

"Trisha, I'm so glad you're home! I hate to ask you at this late date...but my sister was in a car accident...she's *okay*, but she's in the hospital and can't fly over for the wedding..."

Out of her roommate's rather breathless and disorganized account of the situation, Trisha finally gathered that Leslie wanted Trisha to take her sister's place as the single bridesmaid at the small wedding. And was afraid that Trisha's feelings might be hurt because she was being asked as second choice.

But Trisha didn't feel that way. If she had a sister... and a wedding... the sister would be her first choice as bridesmaid, too. "I'd love to do it," Trisha assured her.

In the next three days, Trisha sometimes wished she had a people-copy machine so she could make a few copies of herself and Leslie to get everything done. A fitting for alteration of the bridesmaid's dress, returning the borrowed red dress to Moori, attending a surprise shower given by another friend for Leslie. Rearranging already-crowded displays at The Pink Turtle to make room for newly arrived items and redoing the display in the undersized front window after both a painting and koa wood sculpture were sold out of it. Oh, yes, she would be so *glad* when she could get into that new space in Hugh's building!

At inappropriate moments, Cody's image occasionally intruded, like one television channel trying to cut in on another, and she kept trying to tune him out. The effort wasn't notably successful, and some faint image, like a ghostly presence, always seemed to be hovering in the background. Although Cody's image, with wicked grin and teasing eyes and occasional roar of motorcycle was a bit too sexy and noisy to be classified as truly ghostly.

At the last minute, there was yet another wedding crisis. Tyler's nephew, who was scheduled to be ring bearer, came down with the measles, and the ceremony had to be rearranged to do without him.

But finally, *finally*, a radiant Leslie was coming down the aisle of the small church on her father's arm, and, although the term wasn't generally used to describe a bridegroom, an equally radiant Tyler was waiting for her.

"All brides are beautiful, and all bridegrooms are handsome," Hugh observed later at the small reception, which he attended with Nan, and Trisha agreed.

* * *

Cody arrived at his apartment complex in Vancouver late Monday evening. He was not in a good humor. Attending the reunion on his motorcycle before he did it had seemed like a much better idea than it did now that he'd actually done it. He still enjoyed an occasional afternoon outing on the big bike, but some four hundred and twenty-five miles in one day went beyond the classification of fun.

Tired back and butt were really not what was bothering him most, however. It was Trisha.

He still couldn't figure out what had gone wrong. They'd been having so much fun and getting along so great. He'd even been considering asking if she could postpone her return to Kauai and come to Vancouver to visit for a few days. And then the motel office had called and given him that odd message that she wouldn't be able to have dinner with him, after all, cold and uninformative as a recording on an answering machine.

At first, angry with the unexpected stand up, he'd muttered, *Okay. Fine. The hell with her.* Maybe she'd only been pretending to have a good time. Maybe she'd decided she'd rather wash her hair than see him again. He'd just go out for a hamburger, hit the sheets early and get an early start home in the morning. Papers on the sale of the apartment complex should be ready to sign, and he could start looking around for a good property in which to reinvest the money.

But the cryptic message kept gnawing at him, and after an hour, he'd decided to call Trisha and demand an explanation. After trying every fifteen minutes for another hour, the obvious conclusion was that she wasn't in the motel room. So what did that mean? That she'd gotten a better offer? A thought that only made him more angry.

Then he'd started getting concerned. Maybe she was ill. Maybe she'd received unexpected bad news.

Sitting around fretting and stewing was not the way Cody usually operated. He got on the motorcycle and roared over to the motel.

The first thing he noted was that the slot where her rental car had been parked was empty. Which meant—?

He ran up the stairs to the second-floor balcony and knocked on the door. No answer, which didn't surprise him. By that point, frustration had joined the anger.

A four-inch gap separated the gold-colored drapes at the window of the room. After a moment's hesitation, he cupped his hands around his face so he could peer inside. The bed was unmussed, and he saw no suitcase or personal belongings. And the key was on the nightstand.

She'd walked out. Just like that, no apology, no explanation, no nothing. She'd just picked up and left.

Cody was not a man who had been stood up often, and he did not take it well. The rear tire of the motorcycle branded rubber on the pavement as he squealed out of the parking lot.

On the long ride back to Washington, however, he'd had plenty of time to mull over the situation more calmly, inspecting and examining it from all sides, as he might a piece of property he was considering buying. But no matter how he turned it, he just didn't understand. *Baffled* was the word. He replayed in depth the events of the two days they'd spent together. Had he unknowingly antagonized her in some way? Bored her with the car show and carnival? Come on too strong? Not strong enough? *What?*

His conclusion was that unless she'd been concealing world-class talents as an actress, she'd had just as great a time as he had and he hadn't done anything drastically wrong.

Could it be that she was still holding an old grudge about what had happened when they were teenagers? And decided to pull a little get-even trick? It was possible. Maybe he deserved it. But he couldn't believe that was what she'd done. Trisha was too honest and straightforward for that. There was no deceit in her. If she was still angry with him, she'd simply have told him so. At least that was the kind of person she'd been ten years ago.

He just didn't know what to believe. He'd thought something very special was happening between them. And she'd walked out.

Melissa had left his mail on the desk in the spare bedroom that he used as an office. He riffled through it, efficiently separating it into piles and discarding the junk. He glanced at his watch, thinking he might run across the courtyard to Melissa's apartment and see Debbie for a few minutes and hear how she was doing at her summer day camp. But it was too late for that; she'd be in bed by now. He checked his answering machine, mentally groaning at the overly cute message from a woman named Michelle whom he'd dated a few times. He was more interested in the call from the broker who said the papers on the sale of the apartment were indeed ready to sign. The sale came at a propitious time for looking for reinvestment property, because he wouldn't be returning to work at Mount St. Helens for another five or six weeks. Government budget problems meant that reorganization and funding of the project would delay work at least that long. He might not have even attended the reunion if he hadn't had this extended amount of time off work.

In the refrigerator he found some cookies and a note from Melissa saying she'd baked them in his oven because hers was on the blink. She'd called a repairman but he couldn't come for several days. At the bottom of the note were a couple of lines in his niece Debbie's careful handwriting saying she'd won a prize at day camp for the dragon kite she'd made. He'd helped her get the project started before he left. A P.S. read, Miss Evans is taking us on a picnic to the zoo!

He was really going to miss her, he thought regretfully. But the coming change in Melissa and Debbie's lives would be a great thing for both of them. Marty was a terrific guy. And he should know, he thought wryly. He'd never reveal it to Melissa, of course, but he'd had Marty checked out by the best agency around. David's daughter, and the woman David had loved, deserved the best.

Over the next three days, Cody did more fuming and stewing than he was accustomed to doing over any woman. He was angry and frustrated with Trisha's unexplained departure, in the unaccustomed position of feeling indignant about how a woman had treated him. He was also, although it took him a while to admit it even to himself, a little hurt. Apparently, what had seemed so special to him hadn't been special at all to Trisha.

He kept thinking she might call with some enlightening explanation, but there was no call. There hadn't yet been time for a letter from Hawaii. So she might still write, unless . . .

Possibilities that he'd not before considered suddenly spurted into his mind. If she'd left Horton upset about something, perhaps she'd had an accident. And weird things happened. They were in the news every day. Kidnappings, carjackings, car accidents undiscovered for days. Crazy ex-boyfriends, unbalanced druggies, even irrational classmates. The more he thought, the higher the list of alarming possibilities mounted. Suppose she'd been forced against her will to leave Horton? Suppose she'd never made it back to Kauai?

All of which sounded melodramatic and highly unlikely, especially in small-town Horton. But remotely *possible*.

On Thursday evening, he called the reunion committee chairman and got an address and phone number for Trisha, an action he suspected would be on the gossip circuit within minutes. The time was late, but he dialed Trisha's number, anyway. He wasn't sure of the exact time difference between the mainland and Hawaii, but it would be earlier there. If she'd never made it home, he wanted to know.

The phone rang a good dozen times before a female voice answered. Trisha? He didn't think so, but he couldn't be certain, because the voice sounded so breathless. He spoke her name tentatively. "Trisha?"

"No, she isn't here now." Big breath. "I think maybe she went out to dinner or a party." Another breath. "Sorry. I was just climbing through the kitchen window when the phone started ringing. You might be able to catch her if you call later, about ten-thirty or eleven."

He thought about asking *why* this woman was crawling through Trisha's kitchen window, but then he mentally shrugged it off as irrelevant. "Okay, thanks."

So she wasn't kidnapped or lying in a ditch somewhere. She was safely home, out living it up at a party, not in the least concerned that he was sitting over here worrying about her.

Was he going to call her later, as the breathless-sounding woman suggested? No. The hell with that.

Late Sunday afternoon, Hugh came over to help Trisha move her heavy worktable and set up her jewelry-making workshop in the other, now-empty bedroom. Afterward, Trisha fixed tuna sandwiches, and they ate at the table in the nook that served as a dining area.

"I'm going to have to buy new living room furniture now that Leslie is gone," Trisha remarked as she eyed the empty, flattened spaces on the living room carpet. "Maybe I'll go all out and get new bedroom and dining room furniture, too."

"Mmm." A noncommittal response if there ever was one.

Trisha took a closer look at the man sitting across from her at the slightly lopsided table. Hugh was tall and rangy, with even, good-natured features that sometimes deceived opponents in court into thinking he was a less formidable opponent than he actually was. Just now, however, that good-looking face was as long and sad as that of the teddy bear in her closet. He had seemed distracted and unusually uncommunicative ever since he arrived.

"And then I think I'll start building a flying saucer in the backyard," she added, testing whether or not anything was getting through. "Purple would be a nice color for a flying saucer, don't you think?"

Hugh roused, took a big bite of sandwich and apparently extracted the word saucer out of her facetious statement. "Great. You could use some new dishes."

"Hugh, you're off in another world. Is something wrong? Things not going right with Nan?" Everything had seemed fine at the wedding the previous evening.

"No, everything's great with Nan." He paused a moment. "Well, maybe not *great,* but okay."

"She isn't bothered by our friendship, is she?" Actually, Trisha had introduced Hugh and Nan, and, like any matchmaker, she had a proprietary interest in how the romance worked out. But even in this day, some people, both

men and women, had a difficult time accepting the idea that
a man and woman could just be great friends, as she and
Hugh were.

"Oh, no. She's fine with that."

"How about work on the building?" The building, located in the Kapaa area, was some distance from both Trisha's apartment and The Pink Turtle, and she'd been too
busy to drive up that way since returning from the reunion.

"The work has slowed. Everything takes longer and costs
more than I originally figured. I think I'll stick to law after
this."

Hugh had acquired the commercial structure, badly
damaged in last year's hurricane, in lieu of payment of a
large bill from a client who was both financially strapped
and in a horrendous legal mess. Considering how little attention Hugh often paid to money matters—and how soft-
hearted he often was with down-on-their-luck clients—
Trisha thought he'd done rather well in this situation. He
was having to put a considerable amount of money into re-
pairs and remodeling, but the building should be an excellent money-maker once the various units were ready to rent.
The chance to move into it came at an opportune time for
Trisha, not only because the space was large and well located but also because the building The Pink Turtle now
occupied was going to be turned into a restaurant later this
year. The sportswear shop located next to The Pink Turtle
was also planning to move into Hugh's building.

Hugh stood up abruptly, leaving half the sandwich. That
was definitely unusual for always-hungry Hugh, who had
once, in a more lighthearted mood, said that he thought that
in a previous life he may have been a garbage disposal unit.
"Let's take a walk on the beach. I need some fresh air and
exercise."

Trisha, barefoot, slipped into shoes for the walk to the
beach, then took them off again when they reached the
sand. Hugh asked about the reunion, and she gave him a
sketchy version of it, highlighting the humorous incidents
in hopes of bringing him out of his down mood. He still
seemed distracted, but he managed to laugh in the right
places. She didn't mention Cody, not because he was any big

secret but because she wanted to get the reawakening of her feelings for him, which had surged dangerously close to out of control at the reunion, into perspective before discussing them even with her old friend Hugh.

The outside lights had come on around the two-story apartment building by the time Trisha and Hugh returned from the beach. Trisha hadn't put her shoes on again, and they were still in her left hand. Someone was standing at her door. She could see only a male silhouette, but the tall figure with football-player shoulders slanting to lean hips had an odd familiarity. And there was something about the stance and shape of head as he peered at the nameplate by the doorbell....

No. Surely not. Impossible. Her mind was playing tricks on her, stamping a mistaken identity on a live body simply because his image had dominated her thoughts all day.

The man started to walk away, then turned and punched the doorbell with an impatience that suggested he'd done it several times already.

"Is that someone you know?" Hugh asked.

"I'm...not sure."

They were closer by then, and the man at her door glanced in their direction. When he looked up, the light from the lanterns along the walkway highlighted the planes of his face and the dark gloss of his hair. Trisha stopped short. Looming on her doorstep, unsmiling, formidably muscular, the glitter of his dark eyes flicking between her and Hugh, he looked intimidating, even dangerous. A crazy impulse to start running flashed through her...but she was uncertain if her feet would impetuously hurtle her away or toward that rugged figure.

"Are you looking for someone?" Hugh asked in a pleasant but unintimidated tone. He took a step forward, placing himself protectively between Trisha and what to him was an unknown intruder. Although Hugh was the taller of the two, Cody had about twenty muscular pounds on him.

Cody stepped to the side, to a point where Trisha was again in his line of vision. And he in hers.

"What are you doing here?" Trisha demanded.

"We can discuss that in private." The words were phrased politely but the tone held command, not request.

"Trisha, do you know this man?" Hugh looked at Trisha for some clue as to what was going on here. He still wasn't intimidated, but he sounded less certain of his position as her defender. She tucked her left hand under his arm to make obvious to Cody that she was not about to desert Hugh and accede to Cody's demand for a private discussion.

"This is Cody Malone," Trisha said by way of explanation to Hugh. She kept a wary eye on Cody, uncertain of his intentions, aware again that he was not a predictable man. "He went to Horton High. We happened to run into each other at the recent reunion."

Trisha didn't deliberately not complete the other half of the introduction. In her surprise and agitation, she simply neglected that nicety. One part of her felt an unexpected and totally unwanted pleasurable flowering of surprise that he had come all this way to see her; another part saw the grim look on his face and shivered in apprehension.

Finally, with a pointed glance at Hugh, Cody said, "And this is—?"

Remembering that Cody had just been inspecting the nameplate that still read "Lassiter/Anderson," Trisha, with a sudden flash of inspiration, improvised. "This is Hugh, Hugh Anderson," she said, adding Leslie's last name to Hugh's. She was certain she'd never mentioned Hugh's real last name to Cody. She slammed the side of her knee into Hugh's leg hoping he'd catch the signal and not contradict this wild fabrication. "Hugh Anderson—Cody Malone."

Cody's glance flicked to the nameplate to recheck the names. He apparently didn't need diagrams to figure out what she was saying, that she and "Hugh Anderson" shared the apartment. Hugh looked confused, but he didn't say anything incriminating. The two men shook hands like a couple of prizefighters warily sizing each other up.

"Apparently, there were details of your life here on the island that you didn't bother to mention at the reunion," Cody suggested.

*That makes two of us, then, doesn't it?* Trisha snapped mentally, but all she said aloud was a stiff, "I'm sorry if there was a misunderstanding."

Hugh cleared his throat as if he was about to say something, and to forestall that, she said with manufactured heartiness, "Well, it's been nice seeing you again, but Hugh and I were just on our way to a movie. So if you'll excuse us—" With her hand clamped around Hugh's arm, she more or less propelled him toward his car.

She and Hugh hadn't discussed going to the movies. Trisha had, in fact, planned to spend the evening working on a ring design that a customer had commissioned for her husband, a challenge because most of Trisha's coral designs had been for women's jewelry.

Once in the car, Hugh looked completely bewildered. "What in the hell was all that about?"

Trisha didn't answer for a moment. She waited until she saw Cody walk to a dark car parked down the street and drive away. Then she said, "Oh, he's just this . . . pushy guy from the reunion. Letting him think you and I live together just seemed like a good way to get rid of him."

In the shadowy dimness of the car, Hugh gave her a quick glance. "So how come you're so shook up?"

"I'm not shook up." But she then realized she was unconsciously shredding a tissue from her pocket into a small mountain of fluttery bits. Hastily she gathered the shreds and stuffed them into the litter bag hanging from the knob of the glove compartment. "I'm just surprised at seeing him here so unexpectedly."

"He must have had some reason to think he'd be welcome or he wouldn't have flown across an ocean to see you," Hugh suggested. "You were downright *rude*. That isn't like you."

"I invited a lot of people to look me up if they ever got to Kauai. I had no idea he was going to jump on the first plane and do it," she answered defensively.

So why had he come?

Because she was that rare creature, the woman who got away without being added to his list of successful bedroom conquests? And his male ego demanded he rectify that situation?

Whatever the reason, it didn't matter, she told herself firmly. She'd gotten rid of him.

"So, now that we're here, I'm all for seeing that movie," Trisha added with manufactured enthusiasm.

"To tell the truth, I really don't feel much like a movie. I have some paperwork at home that I ought to tackle."

She didn't argue. "Okay. I'll talk to you sometime during the week, then." She slid out of the car but paused to peer through the window at Hugh. "You're sure everything's okay?"

"Sure. Just a tough case in court tomorrow."

Trisha made a fresh pot of coffee and settled down to work on the ring design. She'd been at it about an hour when the doorbell rang.

Hugh must have decided to come back and tell her what was wrong, because she suspected something was in spite of his assurances to the contrary. She didn't have a peephole, so she had to unlock and open the door to see for certain who was there. She was glad she hadn't removed the security chain when she saw that the man at her door was not Hugh.

"Cody!"

"May I come in?"

"I don't see any point in that."

"This is not exactly the friendly greeting for which Hawaii is famous," he grumbled. "Aren't there supposed to be leis and dancing girls?"

"Sorry. I seem to be fresh out of both."

She started to close the door, but tanned fingers thrust through the narrow opening stopped her. "Trisha, I think you owe me an explanation about why you walked out."

"I don't owe you anything!" Remembering her misleading fabrication of a few minutes earlier, she went on attack by adding, "And what are you doing coming here *now,* at this time of night, interrupting . . . I mean, you know Hugh and I are *living* here together—" She wanted to say that he'd roused her and Hugh out of the intimacy of bed, but she couldn't quite manage that large a story.

"How long have you been living together?" His tone suddenly went polite, almost deferential.

"For... a long time. A *long* time. We're very happy."

"And I suppose Hugh would object if I asked you to dinner because he doesn't like his roommate going out with other men?"

"Yes, that's right. Exactly right. And you wouldn't want to go out with a woman who's... entangled with another man, so..."

Unexpectedly he laughed, the one rogue eye she could see through the narrow opening dancing with wicked mischief. In dismay she realized he'd been leading her on until here she was, floundering in her living-together story like a fish in a teacup. She couldn't figure how, but he knew it was all a wild fabrication.

"Maybe your story would have been more convincing if you'd been wearing shoes," he suggested. "There's something about bare feet that lacks... authority."

Still barefoot, she self-consciously covered one foot with the other, the cinnamon pink toenails somehow looking absurdly frivolous.

"Trisha, darlin', all I did when I got in my car was drive around the block," Cody explained. "When I turned the corner, I saw you getting out of Hugh's car and coming back to your apartment. *Alone.* I've been waiting out there for an hour to see if Hugh also came 'home,' and he hasn't."

"He has meetings. Lawyer meetings." The statement sounded not only feeble but ridiculous, even to her. "And you have no business spying on me!"

"Trisha, I don't think he lives here now or has ever lived here. For one thing, when I called your apartment a few days ago, a woman answered."

"You... called?" Trisha faltered.

"I was concerned. I thought perhaps something disastrous had happened when you disappeared."

"I'm sorry. I didn't mean to worry you. I appreciate your concern—" Then she steeled herself to reject that apologetic line of thought and made a left turn into confronta-

tion. "Perhaps the message I left for you at the motel should
have made more clear that I was in good health and sound
mental condition when I made the decision to skip dinner
with you. Unlikely as it may seem to you that any woman of
sound mind would make such a decision."

He ignored that tart statement. "I didn't leave a message
when I called. The woman I talked to told me to call back
later, that you were at a party, or something."

Usually Leslie had informed her when a man called, even
if he didn't leave a name or message, but it wasn't surprising that she hadn't this time. In the few days before the
wedding, there'd been too much excitement, everything
from the change in bridesmaids to a missing bridal veil and
Leslie's locking herself out of the apartment and having to
crawl through the kitchen window the evening of the surprise shower.

"But you didn't call back."

"No. By then, I knew you were safe, and I decided that
we probably couldn't settle anything on the phone, anyway. So I decided to come in person. Where you also
wouldn't be able to do something such as hang up on me."

"I see. You can just walk away from your job whenever
you want to?"

"The project at Mount St. Helens is undergoing some
reorganization because of budget problems. I'm off for
several weeks."

Again, "I see."

"Trisha, can't I come in? This is a little awkward standing on your doorstep with my fingers wrapped around your
doorjamb."

The fact that he'd been concerned enough about her wel-
fare to call momentarily softened her resistance. But it didn't
really change anything, she reminded herself. He was still
the man who airily juggled women like the star of some
carnival act juggling knives: Melissa in Vancouver, Trisha
in Hawaii, and how many more were there that neither of
them knew about? She was also well aware that, in spite of
her hostility, if he once got inside, there was the potent
danger that under the spell of his seductive persuasions, her
resistance might melt completely. In unacceptable ways.

"No. You can't come in."

"You're still not admitting that guy doesn't live here?" When Trisha, without answering, started to squeeze the door against his fingers, he turned a foot sideways and added the toe of his shoe to his assault on the opening. "It really doesn't make any difference if he lives here or not. I remember your mentioning someone named Hugh, but I'd bet big bucks that his last name isn't Anderson."

Trisha made no comment.

"Trisha, why don't you stop playing games and level with me about what's going on? You owe me two explanations now, one about why you disappeared at the reunion and another about this weird farce tonight."

"I told you, I don't owe you anything!" Trisha flared. "We had a great time at the reunion, but it's over. Let's just leave it at that, okay?"

She was not about to tell him that she'd run out because she was *too* attracted to him, her emotions much too vulnerable, her desires much too potent. Nor was she about to admit that she'd succumbed to his male magnetism, after all, called his home and been zapped by the presence of his playmate Melissa.

"Look, it's getting late, and I have work to do—"

"At this hour of the night?"

"I do most of my jewelry-design work at home. I'm working on a ring for a customer. So if you don't mind—" She applied a little pressure to the door, which had no effect on the grip of his fingers or the thrust of his toe, but he did glance at his watch.

"Okay, it is late," he agreed reluctantly. "We'll continue this discussion at dinner tomorrow night. Even if you don't owe me an explanation, you do owe me your presence at a dinner. You agreed to that."

She was not about to be persuaded by an appeal to some vague standard of etiquette. She didn't bother to make up an excuse about being busy. She simply said, "I don't think so."

"You have a choice. Dinner with me tomorrow night, or I stand here like an incompetent burglar with my toe and fingers caught in your door." He spoke in a conversational tone, but there was no doubt but that he meant what he said. He got a firmer grip on the doorjamb and wedged his foot a little farther into the opening.

She considered the threat. "Until when?"

"Until a passing policeman stops and arrests me or rigor mortis sets in, whichever comes first. Although I may get noisy in the meantime."

Somehow Trisha suspected that even if he didn't last until either of those dire events occurred, he was quite capable of standing there for an embarrassing length of time. And also capable of being noisy, a situation her retired neighbors would not appreciate. She was probably lucky one of them hadn't already popped out, like the man at the motel in Horton.

"Very well," she agreed reluctantly. "Dinner tomorrow night. Although I don't see any point in it. You're...staying somewhere here on the island?"

"Yes, I am. But if you think I'm going to tell you where so you can call and back out, think again." He removed his toe and fingers, and she could see him flexing his fist to relieve the strain. "I'll pick you up at eight o'clock." A statement not a question.

It was against her better judgment, but she didn't seem to have a choice. She nodded. Refusing to lose control of the situation completely, she added, "But I'll meet you at a restaurant."

She named a restaurant in the Kapaa area, not far from Hugh's building, and gave him brief instructions on how to find it. He looked undecided, as if inclined to demand that he pick her up at her door. But finally he nodded, adding a final warning shot before he turned away from the door.

"And don't even think about not showing up."

## Chapter Six

Trisha, in pale orchid bikini panties and lacy bra, stood undecided at the open door of her closet. She didn't want to dress in a manner that suggested this was a real *date* or that she was in any way trying to appear inviting or seductive. But pride dictated that she not go looking like something that had washed up on the beach.

The evening was warm, and she finally chose a conservative shirtwaist dress in a soft cream color. The silky fabric was dressy enough for evening wear, but the casual style would never be considered seductive. She added small earrings of polished pink coral outlined in silver and a two-strand necklace of alternating silver and coral beads.

She gave herself plenty of time to reach the restaurant but halfway there slowed her driving speed. She didn't want to be late, which she thought Cody might misinterpret as some feminine plot to make a dramatic entrance. She remembered that at her door he had accused her of "playing games" with him, and she also didn't want him to think she was coyly playing hard to get. But neither did she want to be early and have it look as if she was *eager* to meet him.

Oh, damn, she thought, suddenly cross with herself. What did she care what he thought about her, one way or the other? She was only meeting him for this dinner because he'd more or less blackmailed her into it.

He was again going to demand to know why she had deserted him at the reunion, and she again had no intention of revealing her reasons. But she also wasn't inclined to repeat last night's ridiculous performance, trying to hide behind some foolish fabrication. Deceit had never been part of her character, and she was not comfortable with any form of it. But stubbornness was a part of her, and that was how she would handle this evening, she decided, by simply digging in her heels and keeping personal matters personal.

They hadn't discussed where at the restaurant to meet, but she saw him standing near the front entryway as she was looking for a parking space. She also saw two attractive women about her own age stop to talk to him. Good ol' Cody, she thought wryly. As irresistible to the opposite sex as ever. Women would find him, or he'd find them, if he were stranded on an ice floe in the Antarctic.

*But I am immune to you, Cody Malone,* she told herself with no-nonsense firmness when she approached the hibiscus-lined walkway a few minutes later. *You were an addiction that trapped me for a while a long time ago... an addiction briefly recycled at the reunion... but now I am cured.* Like a protective mantra she repeated the words. *I am immune to you.*

A protection that really seemed unnecessary as the uncomfortable evening progressed.

A hostess clad in a long, brightly flowered *pareau*—a gown that could be wrapped and tied a dozen different ways—with an orchid in her hair, led them to a booth at the rear of the room. Except for some uninspired palms-and-sea paintings hanging on the tan walls, the hostess's gown was as far as Hawaiian ambience went.

Cody smiled, the first time he'd done so that evening. No smile from Cody could be considered *un*attractive, but this was not one of his more dazzling flashes. "You did not, I see, choose this place on the basis of its romantic atmosphere."

"The food is very good," Trisha returned defensively.

But he was right about romantic atmosphere. She had chosen the restaurant precisely because it had none. No cozy tables, no flattering candles, no dreamy music, no windows overlooking a romantic scene of moonlit sea. The Golden Fisherman catered to local families, not honeymoon couples. It provided good food at moderate prices, with plenty of high chairs and infant seats available. She and Hugh usually came here on the rare times they went out to dinner together.

Trisha pretended to study the menu, although she already knew that she was going to order the teriyaki chicken. Not that she had much appetite for eating anything.

"Did you have a chance to see the island today?" she asked tentatively as she closed the menu.

"I drove up the Waimea Canyon road to the Kalalau Valley Lookout this morning. Incredible scenery. I'm staying at a hotel near Poipu, in what is supposed to be one of the best bodysurfing areas on the island, so I tried bodysurfing this afternoon. An inexpert try, I'm afraid, but fun."

She remembered that at the reunion he had once asked, if he showed up on her doorstep, would she take him hiking and surfing? He did not mention that now.

"I also drove by The Pink Turtle."

"You could have come in," she said, somehow feeling both awkward and ungracious with the way things were going.

He didn't respond to the comment. The waitress arrived and took their orders. Trisha thought about insisting on separate checks but decided that would be making an issue out of something that was really irrelevant, building a Mount Waialeale out of a road bump. Best to simply get through this evening with as little fuss as possible.

Cody handed his menu to the waitress and leaned back against the red vinyl backrest. He got right to the point. "Do you care to discuss why you walked out at the reunion?"

She noted that this time it was a question, not a demand. She also noted that it was asked in an almost negligent way, as if he didn't anticipate a satisfactory answer but didn't particularly care. Last night, although he had shown obvious anger and frustration with her disappearance at the reunion, there had also been a certain playfulness about him. An involvement. He *cared*. Tonight all that was missing.

She twisted her water glass nervously on the dark table. "There really isn't anything to discuss. It simply seemed an appropriate action at the time. I'm sorry if it...inconvenienced you in any way."

"And last night, your effort to make me think that you and Hugh shared the apartment, that was also 'appropriate'?"

"Probably not," she admitted. "The name on the door, Anderson, is my former roommate's last name. I just hadn't gotten around to removing it yet. Hugh's last name is Lawton. He's my lawyer and we're just old and very dear friends."

"How nice. Good friends are indispensable." A hint of mockery told her he suspected that even if she and Hugh didn't live together, there was more to the relationship than platonic friendship. An implication she didn't bother to deny.

Their salads arrived, hers, as she'd requested, with the oil and vinegar dressing on the side so she could use it sparingly.

She looked up once as she was eating and caught his eyes on her. She thought they registered attraction, but it was an impersonal judgment, the same way she might find a lovely sunset pleasing.

"Did you design your earrings and necklace?" he asked.

She touched the beads at her throat, relieved at the change of subject. "Yes. This was one of my earliest efforts in pink coral."

"Very nice. How did you happen to get into jewelry design?"

"I suppose I've always been interested in it. When I was in grade school, I used to make things out of agates and other rocks." She smiled lightly. "The kind of thing dear to a mother's heart, but not good for much of anything else. I took a jewelry-making course in Honolulu after I moved to Hawaii, but it was several years after that before I really started doing it as anything more than a hobby."

"Do you use coral in all your designs?"

"Almost all. But I do use semiprecious gems such as garnet and amethyst occasionally. I've also done a few primitive designs with wood and shells." He didn't ask, but because an awkward silence followed, she added, "The harvesting of coral around Hawaii is regulated by quotas so the areas won't be stripped, as has been done in some other places. Black coral comes from shallower waters, pink and gold from much deeper, usually down around twelve-hundred feet, beyond the depth divers can reach with scuba gear alone. Which makes the pink and gold more expensive and valuable, of course."

"But I'm sure that a good part of the value of any piece is in the design, and you can be very proud of yours."

The comment was flattering, and yet it was given in a totally detached manner. Almost as if all this were a job interview, one in which the interviewer was being kind but had already decided the applicant wasn't going to get the job. Which annoyed her. This dinner was his idea, not hers.

"You mentioned your mother...I don't believe I ever met your parents," he commented. Another polite question. "Do they also live here in Hawaii now?"

"No. They live in a small town in Ohio where my father is manager of a hardware store." Her parents had finally tired of the frequent moves connected with the job her father had held all the years Trisha was growing up, and they had settled permanently in a small town that was not unlike Horton.

"I suppose that means you don't see them often?"

"They fly over about once a year and I went to see them before I went to the reunion."

Such a polite, almost formal conversation, as if they were strangers instead of two people who had been within a caress of becoming lovers at the reunion. She still wanted to know about David's death, when and how it had happened, but the questions seemed too personal to inject into this reserved, aloof conversation.

Their dinners arrived, his steak, her teriyaki chicken, and as they ate, they carried on a desultory conversation about the weather and the various attractions of the island.

Dessert came with the meal, but they both declined it. The evening was beginning to feel like a windup toy that had run down. The final awkward moment came just outside the entrance of the restaurant where they had to go through the formality of a goodbye.

"Thank you for a lovely dinner," Trisha said, a statement that was surely on the meaningless level of "Have a nice day."

He looked at her, his eyes more personal than they'd been all evening. "I'm sorry I forced you into it. My mistake. I've had a lot of time to think since last night, and I finally realized that in walking out at the reunion and pretending to live with Hugh, you were trying to send me a message. And I, like the thick-skulled jerk I've been known to be in the past, just wasn't getting it."

The too-bright glare of the restaurant's walkway lights revealed every handsome feature of his face, the blue eyes, heavy eyebrows and rugged jaw, even the sensuousness in the masculine curve of his lips, and yet there was something closed, almost forbidding about him.

She almost said he was being too hard on himself but instead remained silent. A gentle evening breeze fluttered her skirt, momentarily lifting it high on her thighs, a movement that did not escape his notice. His gaze did not linger, however.

"I thought something very special happened between us at the reunion." With finality in his voice, he added, "But I can see now that I was mistaken. And you're right. You don't owe me explanations about anything."

He was taking all the blame on himself, and yet outside the polite aura of the words, perhaps in tone of voice and level gaze of eyes, she also detected a hint of disappointment. Disappointment in *her,* that somehow she'd failed to live up to his expectations.

For a moment, a rough tide of regret and confusion and uncertainty engulfed her. She almost said, "Let's go somewhere and really talk this through." She even lifted her hand and almost touched his arm.

And then anger and resentment, fueled by an echo of his Melissa's cheerful voice on the phone, returned, and she withdrew the hand without making contact.

He was disappointed in her? The feeling was mutual.

Instead, she said politely, "Will you be returning to the mainland in the morning?"

"No, I'm going to look up my friend who's heading up a new volcanic research project over in the Kilauea area on the Big Island. I believe I mentioned that I don't have to be back at work at Mount St. Helens for several weeks."

"What will you do with the remainder of the time?" She realized this was none of her business, but at the last minute, in spite of the flare of resentment, she was oddly reluctant to let him go.

"I've just sold my apartment complex in Vancouver. I'll probably spend the time looking for a good reinvestment property."

The answer surprised her. He'd mentioned living in what sounded like a rather nice apartment complex. Fairly upscale, with swimming pool, tennis courts and a view of the mountain where he worked. But he hadn't mentioned *owning* the complex.

She was also puzzled. Such a property surely didn't come cheaply, and she wouldn't have thought being a volcanologist was any way to quick wealth. His family certainly hadn't had much in Horton. Their home, an old-fashioned house with front porch, was modest, in need of a paint job, and the grass in the yard was worn to bare dirt from heavy use of the basketball hoop nailed to the side of the garage. The only time she'd been inside the house, the dining room table was covered with motorcycle parts, not fine china.

He glanced at his watch, the preliminary to goodbye in any language or setting.

"I hope you find your friend over on the Big Island," she offered. "And have a safe trip home."

"Thank you. And the best of luck to you and The Pink Turtle."

He politely waited for her to take the first actual parting steps. She didn't look back when she heard him turn in the opposite direction.

Trisha was more upset than she'd expected to be as she drove away. Her emotions were fuzzy. There was anger, but it wasn't a righteous blaze, and it was tangled with disappointment and regret, resentment, even a vague feeling of guilt.

She headed for home but then remembered that she wanted to look at the progress on Hugh's building. Perhaps she could move The Pink Turtle into her reserved space before renovation of the entire building was completed.

She retraced her route and drove past the Golden Fisherman. She turned into the building's parking area and then braked in surprise. Almost nothing had been done since the last time she'd been there. Metal scaffolding still climbed the walls, but there was no sign of the contractor's equipment and the general clutter of construction work. The place looked deserted, abandoned.

She called Hugh as soon as she got home. What he had to say was distressing, to say the least. Renovation costs had skyrocketed far beyond his expectations. He'd come up short of money when a payment to the contractor was due, and the contractor had walked off the job.

"I am, to put it bluntly, in one hell of a financial mess. The contractor will undoubtedly put a lien against the building. To add to the mortgages already on it."

"Can't you refinance the project?" He'd helped her find her way through the maze she'd encountered when she needed financing to buy The Pink Turtle. "Get your loans extended? Find a new contractor?"

"I've checked every angle and looked into everything I can think of, and I just don't see any way out except to sell the building as quickly as I can and get out before I sink into a worse financial mess than I'm in now."

"But with the renovation still incomplete... won't finding a buyer be rather difficult?"

"I'll have to put the price down to where I *can* sell it. It'll be a good deal for someone, because I'll have to take a big loss on it in order to make a quick sale. I'm really sorry, Trisha. I know this will upset your plans. I've been intending to tell you ever since you got back from the reunion that there were problems, but I kept thinking maybe I could find a way out."

That was Hugh, of course. Never too wrapped up in his own problems to be concerned about someone else's. And this could, as he said, disrupt her plans. Her lease on the present location expired in a couple of months and she had to be out by then. But she could find space elsewhere for The Pink Turtle if she had to, or perhaps even negotiate for space with a new owner of Hugh's building. So it was no insurmountable disaster for her. But it was definitely a huge blow for Hugh.

"What happens if you can't sell it?"

"Do they still have debtors' prisons?" he asked with a hollow laugh.

"I don't think so, but you're the lawyer."

"And I should have stuck with lawyering."

For a moment, she was annoyed with him. If he'd been a better businessman, he wouldn't have gotten bogged down in this problem. He should have investigated renovation costs more thoroughly before accepting the equity in the damaged building as payment of his client's bill. It now looked as if the client may have slid out from under one of his problems by dumping it on Hugh. But that, too, was Hugh. He always took his clients' problems personally...as he had once done hers when she was down-and-out.

"I'm going to talk to a broker tomorrow." Worry over all this, she realized, was undoubtedly what had made him so uncommunicative and distracted when he'd come over to help move her worktable the evening Cody had shown up. "I'll let you know what he says."

"Okay. If there's anything I can do to help, let me know."

"Just bring me a rich buyer with buckets of money." The laugh was still hollow.

She hung up, Hugh's words unexpectedly reminding her that she did know a buyer with money. She had no idea if Cody had "buckets" of it, but she did know he'd just sold his apartment complex in Vancouver and was planning to look for property in which to reinvest the money.

She rejected the thought as soon as it appeared on her mental horizon. A preposterous idea. Cody wouldn't be in-

terested in buying property on Kauai; it was an ocean away
from his home and work. And she wasn't interested in any
further involvement with *him*.

Yet, if it would help Hugh...

She struggled with the idea for a couple of hours, through
washing out panty hose and looking for some photos she
wanted to send in response to a handful Dawn had sent her.
She rejected the idea half a dozen times. The possibility that
Cody might be interested in buying the building was too remote to make contacting him worthwhile. She had no idea
if Cody's apartment complex and Hugh's commercial
building were anywhere near comparable in value. If she did
contact him, perhaps he'd misinterpret it as a feminine ruse
to resurrect some kind of personal relationship between
them. She didn't, in fact, even know *how* to contact him;
he'd never told her where he was staying.

But the question finally came down to, was she going to
put her own reluctance to contact Cody ahead of a possible
chance, remote though it might be, to help Hugh find a solution to his problems?

She could use the same technique of finding Cody here on
Kauai that he'd used to find her in Horton....

Finally, even though it was getting late, she called Hugh
back and told him about Cody, at the same time hastily
adding all the reasons she doubted this idea would work. A
new one suddenly occurred to her; perhaps Cody would
high-handedly reject the deal simply because she was connected with it.

"Let's give *him* a chance to decide if he's interested and
if he has the money to swing the deal." She could hear the
hope in Hugh's voice. "As I told you before, it's going to be
a terrific buy for someone. It might as well be your friend
Cody."

"Okay, I'll try to get in touch with him before he leaves
the island."

"Great. Keep me posted, okay? And thanks. Hey, I just
thought of something. If I can deal with him direct, before
I list it with a broker, I can save paying a big sales commission! Trisha, you just don't know how much I appreciate
this." Hugh's tone was now so buoyant that she halfway

regretted even suggesting this to him—it was such a wild possibility, with so little chance of success.

She *had* suggested it, however, and the next problem was following through and finding Cody.

She had only to look in the Yellow Pages of the phone book to realize finding Cody on Kauai was going to be a much larger task than his had been finding her in Horton. The list of tourist accommodations on the island was daunting. Still, he had mentioned that he was staying in the Poipu area, so that narrowed it down a little.

She spent a good hour with the phone book, laboriously extracting the name and phone number of every hotel, motel, resort and inn with an address in the Poipu area, occasionally checking a map when she was uncertain of the location of a street or road name. By the time she finished, it was too late to try to call him. Rousing him from sleep was probably not a good way to start a sales pitch. But perhaps she could at least find out if he was registered at any of the places on her list.

Her living room was still bare of furniture, so she sat cross-legged on the carpet, phone on her lap, and started dialing.

Cody shaved, showered and dressed. There were frequent interisland flights throughout the day, so he didn't have to rush to catch a plane over to the Big Island, as the island named Hawaii, for which the chain itself was named, was known here. He wanted to pick up a present to take home to Debbie, and something for Melissa, too. He might even buy one of those flamboyant aloha shirts for himself. He'd originally planned to buy presents for both Debbie and Melissa at The Pink Turtle, but he had no intention of following that plan now.

He opened his suitcase, then decided to go down to breakfast before packing. He took a moment to appreciate the view from his third-floor window first. Turquoise blue water, with a scroll of white surf where it met golden sand, picturesque fringe of ironwood where sand joined grass, tall palms. A couple of bodysurfers were already enjoying the translucent waves. Directly below him, the hotel's gardens blazed with hibiscus and a graceful drape of bougainvillea, and a mosaic of dolphins decorated the bottom of the swimming pool.

He liked Hawaii. He liked the feel of the balmy air, the friendly people...minus one not-so-friendly one...and the spectacular scenery. He'd like to take a leisurely helicopter flight over the inaccessible areas of the island, hike the Na Pali trail he'd read about last night in a tourist brochure, take in a luau, see a fire-knife dance, lie on the beach and watch the moon come up. He'd have liked to do all those things with Trisha, dammit.

He felt frustrated with her, himself and this trip, and frustration was not an emotion with which he was comfortably familiar. He tended to set a goal and go after it, and that hadn't worked with Trisha.

Trisha. She was beautiful, no doubt about it. The pale golden hair that made him want to tangle his fingers in the lush shimmer. The hazel eyes that made him want to arouse a happy dance of golden flecks in their green-brown depths. The tempting mouth that he both wanted to kiss and make laugh. The figure, slim and willowy but sweetly rounded in all the right places, that gave him even more intimate ideas. But he'd apparently credited her with character traits that she didn't possess, a straightforward honesty being one of them. He'd quickly unveiled her little deception about living with the lawyer Lawton, but he still didn't know why she'd done it. Nor why she'd walked out at the reunion.

*Women,* his father used to say, adding, with accuracy if not originality, *can't live with 'em, can't live without 'em.*

Well, Trisha was one he could live without. Actually, he thought with another flash of frustration, he hadn't much choice.

He had a hand on the doorknob when the phone on the nightstand rang. Surprised, he returned to answer it.

"Cody?"

He stiffened slightly at the sound of her voice. Although she was the only person he knew on the island, she was still the last person he expected to hear from. "Yes?"

"This is Trisha. I'm sorry to bother you so early, but I wanted to catch you before you left the island."

"As you can see, I'm still here," he answered warily, not knowing what to make of this unlikely call.

"This isn't a personal call." Her tone momentarily bordered on sharp, apparently to make certain he didn't read something into the call that wasn't there. "It's a business matter."

"I see. And what sort of business might *we* have to transact?"

She ignored the small sarcasm in his tone and went on to explain that the owner of the building into which she was planning to relocate The Pink Turtle had just informed her that he had decided to sell the building. Cody had mentioned that he was planning to look for property in which to invest the proceeds from the sale of his apartment complex, and she thought perhaps this building would interest him. It was undergoing renovation at present, but the owner had indicated he was eager to sell and would give a buyer a very good deal.

Up to that point, she'd sounded brisk and self-confident, but the confidence seemed to falter a little when she added, "Of course, I realize you probably aren't interested in buying property here, so far from home, but I just thought I'd mention it to you...."

"I hadn't really considered looking at property here," he agreed. Although he could see that it was an attractive, growing area, and might indeed be an excellent place in which to invest. Japanese buyers, he knew, had invested heavily in Hawaiian property. "But I might be interested. What can you tell me about the building's condition, how much work remains to be done, square footage, price, etcetera?"

"Not much," she admitted. "I was just going to see if you would even consider buying in this area first, and then if you'd like to look at the building."

"Perhaps I should talk to the broker handling the sale."

"I don't think the building has been listed with a broker yet. The only reason I happen to know about the owner's change of plans is that he is notifying people who had reserved space in the building that completion of the renovation might be delayed. Or a new owner might have different ideas about use of the building."

"I wonder what brought about this sudden change in the owner's plans?"

"I . . . really couldn't say."

The possibilities in the deal were intriguing. There was the chance of making an excellent buy if the owner of the building was really anxious to sell, but Cody was a little wary of detouring the usual sales route through a reputable real estate broker. And it was rather odd that the owner had decided to sell right in the middle of renovation. It indicated there might be problems.

"I'll give it some thought," he said finally. "I'm planning to fly over to the Big Island right after breakfast, but if I decide I'm interested in seeing the building or finding out more about it, I'll return to Kauai and give you a call."

"You can't be more definite than that?"

"No. I'm sorry. I didn't have a chance to talk to my friend Al, but I left a message so he's expecting me today. I've also already called home and said I'd be there by the end of the week—"

"Melissa?"

"Yes. I talked to her last night, so she's expecting me."

"I see." If Trisha's tone were any cooler, he'd have ice crystals stuck in his ear, Cody thought. Which annoyed him. He was under no obligation to look at the building just because he had some money to invest. It also occurred to him that Trisha must have put considerable effort into locating him in order to make this phone call, because he hadn't told her where he was staying. None too tactfully he added, "Is there a commission or something in this for you?"

"No!" There was enough outraged anger in the word to remind him of a younger Trisha battering him about the head and shoulders with an oversize book of Shakespeare. He thought she was going to hang up, but then he realized she was just taking a deep breath to calm herself. "I simply thought you might be interested. Thank you for listening. I'm sorry if I delayed your breakfast."

"I see. Well . . . thank you for thinking of me. I'll let you know if I want to see the building."

He had eaten breakfast, packed, turned in his rental car at the airport and was on the plane before a puzzling thought occurred to him. He was reasonably certain he had never mentioned Melissa to Trisha. He didn't think he'd even mentioned Debbie. Not that they were any secret, of course, but mentioning them inevitably brought up questions about his brother David, and David and his father and the accident were still, even after all these years, a painful and disturbing subject for him to discuss.

He reran the last part of the telephone conversation with Trisha through his mind. He was almost certain now that there'd been something odd about the way she said Melissa's name after he'd mentioned calling home. Sarcasm? He couldn't figure how, but was it possible Trisha had gotten some mistaken idea about who Melissa was and what his relationship with her was?

It was an unlikely thought, and yet it nagged at him at odd moments during the next two busy days on the Big Island. He helped his friend Al and the research team move and set up their equipment in a different location in the area of the Kilauea volcano. He'd gotten his pilot's license shortly after finishing college, adding helicopter training later, and his expertise came in handy now. Kilauea had been quite active for several years now, sending rivers of glowing lava all the way to the sea at times, although it was at the moment just sullenly simmering.

On the third day, Cody abruptly decided to return to Kauai. Two reasons. One to check out the building Trisha had told him about. The other to check out Trisha herself.

# Chapter Seven

Cody called Trisha at The Pink Turtle from a phone at the airport.

"Yes, the building is still available," she said in answer to his first question. "However, I understand that the owner has it listed with a real estate broker now, so you can contact him. Just a moment and I'll look up the phone number for you—"

"I want *you* to show me the building."

"I don't have any more information about it than I had earlier."

"I'd prefer to take a first look without the pressure of some big sales pitch from a real estate salesman," he improvised. He also wanted to talk to her, but he didn't mention that for fear of somehow scaring her off.

"You can find the building easily enough yourself. It's not far from the Golden Fisherman where we had dinner." She hesitated and apparently, although with some reluctance, changed her mind. "Although I suppose I could show it to you. If you don't mind waiting until I close The Pink Turtle, about five-thirty?"

"That will be fine."

They arranged to meet in the parking lot of the Golden Fisherman at six o'clock. Before that time, Cody rented a car, found a room within a few steps of the beach and had a quick swim. He also, feeling optimistic about the evening, asked the desk clerk at his hotel for the name of the most romantic restaurant on the island. She considered the question thoughtfully, taking a full minute to come up with a name, and it wasn't until later, after he said thanks and walked away, that he realized her quickly concealed look of disappointment meant she'd thought the question was a preliminary to his asking *her* out. His sensitivity radar could still use some work, he thought ruefully.

He dressed in old jeans for the meeting with Trisha, because when he looked at a property, he liked to look in places a seller didn't necessarily expect an investor to look. When she arrived at the Golden Fisherman, she didn't get out of her car, just motioned to him to follow her. He took a quick glance at the two-story structure when he turned into the parking area behind her. It wasn't ancient but it was a number of years from new. The building was obviously undergoing renovation, as she'd said, but it looked as if the work had stopped midproject.

Then it was Trisha alone who drew his attention. She looked like a sophisticated angel when she stepped out of her car. Slim-skirted white suit, pale golden hair twisted into a knot at the back of her head, amethyst earrings that matched the glimpse of silky blouse at her throat.

She was a very businesslike angel, however. She pointed out the roomy corner space she planned to lease for The Pink Turtle and said that she knew at least one other space on the main floor had also been reserved. "I believe the present owner planned to lease the upper floor as offices, but I don't know if there were any definite commitments made yet. The renovation had to be done not because the building was crumbling but because it was heavily damaged in a hurricane that hit the island last year."

"Was an upper story destroyed?"

"No. Two stories is the original height of the building. As you may have noticed, we don't have the tall buildings here that you see in Honolulu. A height limit was instituted on Kauai some years ago."

He nodded. An excellent idea to protect the scenic beauty. "It looks as if work on the building has stopped. I wonder why."

"You'll have to discuss that with the broker."

He stepped off the dimensions of the building to get a rough idea of the square footage and gingerly made his way through the main floor and basement, getting down on his knees and crawling into a few hard-to-reach places. The basic structure of the building appeared solid and the renovation work done so far showed careful workmanship, but he'd have an expert make a more thorough appraisal if he decided he was really interested.

"No, I don't know the price," Trisha said in answer to that question when he returned to the car. She wasn't dressed for crawling around in unfinished buildings and hadn't accompanied him. "Again, you'll have to talk to the broker. But I got the impression the owner would listen to any reasonable offer."

"I can't say that I'm overly excited about the building. It still needs a lot of work. But I think I'll stick around for a few days and investigate it more thoroughly. I'll call Melissa this evening and tell her I'll be delayed for a few days."

If the name meant anything to Trisha, she was too poised to let it show.

"I don't know if I mentioned Melissa when we were at the reunion," he added with carefully planned casualness. "She's my brother David's widow." Technically that wasn't accurate, but he'd always felt Melissa was David's widow no matter what the legal situation. "And mother of his little girl, Debbie. Debbie's eight now, a terrific kid. Would you believe she was right out there handing me tools when I was rebuilding that '57 Chevy I worked on last year? I can still beat her at darts, but I don't know for how much longer."

Trisha's lips parted and her hazel eyes widened, and he knew he was on to something here. After a long pause, she said, "They live... in your apartment?"

"In my apartment complex, but not in my *apartment*." Where the hell had she gotten that wrong idea? "We've both arranged to keep our apartments for a while after the sale."

Trisha looked uncharacteristically dazed. "I didn't know any of that."

Bluntly he asked, "What did you think?"

"Cody, I—I called your apartment from San Francisco before I flew home. A woman who said her name was Melissa answered. I thought—I mean, she sounded as if she *belonged* there."

"She takes care of my mail when I'm gone. And comes in to water my plants. Maybe I wasn't home from the reunion yet."

"She said you'd be home soon. The television was on. And she was baking *cookies*." Trisha sounded a little frantic, as if she was beginning to realize she'd made a big mistake, but surely the cookies proved something incriminating about Melissa's presence.

He thought back for a moment. "Yeah, that's right, she did come over one evening to bake cookies. Something went wrong with her oven, and she and Debbie had to make cookies for Debbie to take to day camp. A picnic at the zoo I think it was. If she was there Melissa probably would have picked up the phone if it rang. But I don't remember Melissa mentioning that someone called." Although she could have mentioned a call from a woman and he'd just shrugged it off as unimportant. "You didn't leave your name?"

"I . . . hung up."

"Why did you call?"

"I just wanted to apologize and say I'd . . . enjoyed seeing you again. But when she answered I thought it meant you and she were living together."

Good Lord, no wonder he hadn't heard from her!

"You thought wrong," he said bluntly. He hesitated a moment and then said honestly, "Briefly, several years ago, Melissa and I did think it would be great if we could get together. We felt close, both of us having loved and lost David. And both of us loving Debbie. If we were a real family, I could be a full-time father to Debbie. And Melissa is a sweet and wonderful woman and a terrific mother. But somehow we could never get past a big-brother, little-sister feeling for each other. So, in the past few years, we have been family for each other, but not a man-woman sort of family. Melissa is getting married this fall, and then she and Debbie will be moving to California with her new husband. I'm really going to miss them. But I'm happy for them, too. Debbie gets along great with him, and I know it's best for both of them.''

Trisha studied him, as if giving herself a moment to absorb all this and readjust her thinking to encompass what was obviously totally unexpected information. ''You've never told me about David.''

He was glad she'd asked now, out here in the open air and sunshine. ''He and my father were both killed in an avalanche when they were cross-country skiing in Colorado.'' His eyes briefly rose to the lush green slope of Mount Waialeale, so different from the frozen, snowy mountains where he had lost them.

''Oh, Cody, not your father, too!'' Sympathy and compassion shone in the green-brown depths of her eyes.

Cody swallowed, a painful memory momentarily sweeping over him as the avalanche itself had once done. The terror and panic... the frantic digging... the numbing realization of loss....

''Look, I just remembered I want to check on the...access to the second floor. Would you excuse me? I'll be back in a minute.''

He wasn't really concerned about whether the second-floor access was stairs or elevator, but checking gave him a few minutes to stabilize his thoughts and put the past back where it belonged. He still had to do that once in a while. There was more he should tell her, of course, but that could wait.

By the time he returned to the parked cars, he was feeling back to normal. ''Needs a *lot* of work,'' he said, repeating his former statement as he wiped dusty hands on his jeans. ''Although it ought to be a solid, attractive building when it's finished.''

She had written the broker's name and phone number on a card and now she handed it to him. He opened his wallet and slipped the card inside, undecided yet whether he'd contact the broker for more information. Actually, he was a hell of a lot more interested in Trisha than in the building.

"If I asked you to dinner, no threats involved, would you be interested?"

She smiled. Pure angel. "Try me and see."

"I don't intend to take you to the Golden Fisherman," he warned.

The faintest of blushes tinged her cheeks, but there was a wonderful teasing sparkle to her eyes when she said, "I know a hot dog cart that has terrific chili dogs. All we have to do is find out where it's parked today—"

He laughed. "I'll take that as a *yes* to dinner. I'll have to go back to my room and change out of these jeans." The knees were smeared with oil or grease he'd picked up somewhere when crawling around the building. "Then I'll pick you up about eight?"

He thought he detected a slight moment of hesitation, as if she was thinking about meeting him away from the apartment again, a ploy that he recognized would rule out any awkwardness at her door at the end of the evening. He was ready to make crossed-heart promises about best behavior, but she simply said, "Eight o'clock will be fine."

It occurred to him as they drove off in separate vehicles that this still didn't explain why she'd disappeared after the reunion. She hadn't suspected anything about Melissa then, so there must have been some other reason. He could ask her at dinner—

No. He abruptly abandoned that thought. Let it go. It was unimportant, a minor misstep along the path. The pathway to—what? True love?

*Let's not rush things,* he told himself.

But he didn't intend to let any more missteps happen.

Trisha showered, put on fresh makeup and blow-dried her hair into a loose, swingy style. The dress she chose wasn't as daring as the red one she'd borrowed from Moori for the reunion dance, but neither was it as conservative as the sensible shirtwaist she'd worn to her previous dinner with Cody.

The nipped waist did nice things for her figure, and the sunrise pink color brought a glow to her lightly tanned skin. A generous ruffle concealed that the neckline dipped a bit low. She felt warmly feminine in the dress. Not seductive . . . but not exactly *unseductive*, either.

She called Hugh to tell him that Cody had looked at the building but didn't seem too impressed.

"He's leaving right away?" Hugh said.

"No. I think he's going to stay a few more days. We're going out to dinner tonight."

"Hey, great! Give him a sales pitch, will you? Tell him it's the most fantastic deal he'll ever make in his life. That he can buy it and rent it out, as I was planning to do, or just resell it after the renovations are done. And either way, he'll make zillions."

"Zillions?"

"An inexact number describing a generous profit."

"I think I've already done all I can," Trisha protested. "I showed him the building and gave him your real estate broker's name and phone number."

"Trisha, this is really important to me," Hugh said, his tone losing its forced lightness and turning unexpectedly urgent. "*Really* important."

"Well, I'll see if a good time comes up to mention it again."

Actually, Trisha had said all she really wanted to say about the building. She'd wanted to help Hugh by telling Cody about it, but she didn't really want to try to influence him. It was now simply up to Cody to decide if he was interested in buying.

She was rather surprised at the speed with which Hugh had listed the property with a broker, however. She'd thought he'd wait to see if Cody was interested in buying, in hopes of avoiding a big sales commission as he'd said, but he'd contacted a broker as soon as Trisha told him she didn't know if Cody would even return from the Big Island to look at the building. She hadn't intended to get further involved, but in the middle of talking to Cody, she'd decided it might help Hugh if she made certain Cody actually did look at the property. And now, of course, she was so glad she'd done that. Otherwise, she'd never have found out just how mistaken she had been about Melissa!

She was just as attracted to Cody as she had been at the reunion. Okay, admit it, she laughed at herself as she changed to long dangling earrings of pink coral and freshwater pearls. Even more attracted now. Knowing he'd been a father figure to his niece gave her a new perspective on him. She also admired and respected his feelings for his brother's widow and the responsible way in which he had handled those feelings. Cody Malone was indeed a much different person than the teenage heartthrob he'd been at Horton High. Now he was a mature and responsible man ... and still lacking nothing in the heartthrob department.

And he was leaving in a few days.

That fact was enough to remind her that there was still a danger of getting in too deep both physically and emotionally, and she must be careful. But here on her home territory she felt more in control than she had at the reunion.

As a last-minute precautionary measure, however, when the doorbell rang, she rearranged the ruffle on the neckline of the dress to conceal all trace of seductive cleavage.

She also decided, feeling a light breeze when she opened the door, to take along an evening wrap. She invited Cody inside while she went to her bedroom closet for the fringed white silk shawl. While there, she saw an ear of that teddy bear sticking out of the box where she had stuffed it.

*Okay, you can come out and look around for a while,* she told the teddy bear as she removed him from the box and set him by her mirror. *But don't let that give you ideas that it's a permanent arrangement.*

Cody was still standing by the front door when she returned. Actually, that was all he could do, given the state of her still-bare living room.

"You have something against furniture?" he inquired.

She laughed. "No. I just haven't had time to buy any since my roommate moved out and took hers."

"Maybe I could help."

"You wouldn't want to waste your time on the island looking at furniture. There are much more interesting things to do."

"I wouldn't consider it a waste of time."

"Well, we'll see."

He laughed. "Now you sound like Melissa when Debbie wants to do something that Melissa isn't inclined to let her do."

Which was true. She intended to buy not only living room furniture but a new bedroom set, as well, and she had no intention of giving Cody ideas by inviting him along to help select a new bed.

They went to a restaurant at the north end of the island. Cody said he'd called for reservations, but she saw his small frown when they were led to an exposed table in the center of the dimly lit room. There was a brief, hushed-tone discussion, a discreet gesture of something changing hands, and then they were shown to a different table.

This table was enclosed by a private semicircle of glass overlooking the ocean, privacy further ensured by an interior divider of green foliage, and it had all the romantic ambience the Golden Fisherman lacked. A candle burned in an antique holder beside a fresh bouquet of hibiscus. Crystal sparkled on the table, and gleaming silverware bracketed an intricately folded white napkin. Hawaiian guitars strummed in the background, their romantic music soft as the melodic whispers of tropical breezes. Outside, huge north-shore breakers crashed against dark rocks below their window, their roar silenced by the heavy glass.

"Better than a hot dog cart?" Cody asked lightly. He was wearing light blue slacks and a dark blue jacket that emphasized the rugged breadth of his shoulders.

"Better than a hot dog cart," Trisha echoed with a smile. At one time, she'd have found the expensive setting intimidating, but now she could simply enjoy it. "You didn't just call the first restaurant your finger happened to hit in the phone book," she suggested.

"No. I inquired around for the name of the most romantic restaurant on the island."

"I see." She tilted her head. "And why the most romantic?"

"Why not?" he returned with a teasing gleam of blue eyes.

Trisha had the mahimahi fish, flaky and tender, Cody the prawns in an herb-and-butter sauce, and they laughed with the conspiratorial demeanor of children as they shared bites in the luxurious privacy of their glassed-in semicircle. They had white wine with dinner, and coffee with the airy coconut mousse. They talked about everything and nothing. And, in spite of his stated demand for romantic atmosphere, he kept her laughing with tales about his various travels, including one about the elderly woman who sat next to him on the return flight from the Big Island.

"She was such a sweet, grandmotherly-looking little lady, sitting there writing postcards. She asked what I did, so I asked what she did, expecting to hear about her grandchildren. Instead she said, 'I write horror stories about vampires.' Then she gave me this lovely smile and added, 'Some of the most ordinary-looking people in the world are vampires, you know.' So then she looked at *me,* and I looked at *her....*"

Trisha laughed and told him about the customer at The Pink Turtle who bought a very expensive pair of earrings for herself and then ordered a second pair exactly like them for her Doberman. "Or maybe it was the other way around," she said on second thought, and laughed. And then there was the artist who tried to interest her in handling his "condiment" paintings done in ketchup and mustard and soy sauce.

They also talked about his trip to the Big Island. "Scientists don't believe in Pele, I suppose?" Pele was the mythical goddess of the volcano. In her primitive-design jewelry, Trisha occasionally used a semiprecious volcanic stone known as olivine, also sometimes called "Pele's tears."

Cody laughed. "No. But that didn't keep me from tossing her a candy bar as an offering. Just in case."

Afterward, they went dancing at three different places, changing scenes not because one was unsatisfactory but because the night felt wonderfully endless, too big and exciting to be contained in one spot. They danced to fast music and slow, to dreamy Hawaiian guitars and a hot Latin beat. Sometime after midnight, Cody took off his jacket and tie, and they both kicked off their shoes and walked barefoot on the beach in the moonlight. Trisha showed him one of her favorite places, where a spotlight on the beach targeted a section of surf where some underwater obstruction turned each wave into a glittering explosion of white water.

Cody was leaning against a slanting palm tree, his arms curved around her from behind, hands clasped at her waist as they watched the spotlit surf. She leaned back against him, her head against his shoulder, enjoying the warmth of his body against her back. She was recklessly glad she'd left her evening shawl in the car so she had an excuse to snuggle deep into the enclosing cave of his body and arms.

Occasionally, his lips nuzzled the side of her throat, each touch sending a delicious tingle curling like a slow-motion electric current through her body. She could follow its progress through her skin and body, ending somewhere deep and low inside her. When his teeth gently nipped her earlobe, the electric current was no longer slow and lazy; it sizzled and flashed in a series of small, hot explosions.

"Turn around, Trisha," he whispered.

He didn't turn her, merely loosened his arms a fraction of an inch, so the choice was hers. And she made that choice, turning to wrap her arms around his neck and mold her body against his, leaning forward to make up for the backward slant of his body.

Her back was to the moon, full glow of its light on his face. His eyelids were half-closed, his gaze on her mouth. He moved his head forward but stopped short of her lips. His eyes lifted to hers.

"Aren't you going to meet me halfway?" he challenged.

Oh, yes... yes, yes, she thought as she lifted her mouth to his.

It was a kiss of sweet tenderness heated with a fiery core of passion. His lips wedded hers in a heady blend of softness and strength, and his tongue tantalized her with advance and retreat. One hand caressed her back but the other moved lower, holding her to him until she felt an unfamiliar ache spreading through her.

She pulled her mouth away from his. "Cody," she whispered, uncertain if it was a plea for more or less.

He dipped his head and kissed her where the ruffled neckline of her dress concealed the upper curve of her breasts. He nuzzled the ruffle aside, his tongue tracing a circle of exquisite heat in the intimate cleft of her breasts. Shakily, she did pull away.

He straightened up, not releasing her but loosening the hot weld of their bodies.

"Sorry." He grinned, a moonlit flash more teasing than apologetic. He lifted a hand and rearranged the ruffle into its more decorous position. "It's just that I've been eyeing that particular spot all evening and couldn't resist any longer."

He took her home then. All the way, she rehearsed how to handle the potentially awkward situation when they reached her apartment, certain that Cody had ideas that went beyond ending the evening at the door. But under the amber lights, where she had first seen him impatiently punching her doorbell, he simply said, "Thanks for a wonderful evening, Trisha. I hope you enjoyed it as much as I did."

He kissed her, but it was a chaste kiss, undemanding. She felt momentarily confused, panicky in a way she hadn't expected to be. This was not what she had rehearsed. Didn't he want to see her again? So what came out was a stumbling question about the building. "Are...you planning...to talk to the broker tomorrow?"

"Yes, I probably will. But, considering the potential cost of the renovations, the price would have to be really low to interest me."

Taking courage in hand, she asked the question that was more important to her. "Will I see you again before you leave?"

"That's up to you."

"Dinner tomorrow night? Here? Seven o'clock? Spaghetti?" It all came out in a rush.

Cody grinned. "Yes...yes, yes and yes. I'll bring wine and french bread?"

"Yes."

Cody contacted the broker the next morning, and the price on the building surprised him. It was indeed lower than he had anticipated, although the estimate from the contractor on what completion of the renovations would cost was less attractive. The financing was also a mess, with foreclosure threatened on a couple of loans against the property. That didn't concern him too much, because he had the proceeds from the sale of the apartment complex and could probably clean up the problems with cash. Still, he wasn't eager to get involved in lengthy legal complications. He wasn't some hard-driving tycoon who reveled in nasty negotiations.

He went back to the building and gave it another inspection. Afterward, he bought a bottle of red wine recommended by a clerk who seemed knowledgeable, and a loaf of crusty french bread. From a street vendor, he added a bouquet of some unfamiliar but sweet-smelling lavender flowers.

He was pleased with how happy Trisha was to see him when he arrived at her apartment door. She didn't try to hide her feelings behind some coy show of indifference, like a few women he'd known.

The apartment smelled wonderful, the scent of spaghetti sauce rich with tomatoes and spices, and she smelled wonderful, too, when he dropped a quick kiss on her cheek. A subtle hint of fresh-smelling shampoo and soap, with just a touch of some light cologne.

"Mmm, jacaranda," she said, lifting the graceful, bell-shaped flowers to her face. Though the flowers were beautiful, they dimmed in comparison to the glowing face touching them. "I'll get a vase."

She found a white vase and set the flowers on the table in the tiny area that served as dining room. He eyed the table, and she laughed.

"Yes, you're right, it is lopsided. Also a little lower than most tables."

"I might be able to level it for you."

"Hugh tried that. He cut a little off one leg, then another and another. By the time he was on the second round, I stopped him before I wound up with an ankle-high table."

She picked up the bottle of wine. "Is this a kind that is supposed to be served chilled or at room temperature?"

"Beats me," he said cheerfully.

"But I thought you were a wine expert. You picked such a perfect white wine to go with our dinner last night."

"Sheer luck," he admitted. "I just pointed to one and hoped for the best."

Cody never tried to present himself as something other than what he was to any woman, but with Trisha he felt especially comfortable. He was glad he'd taken her to the romantic, luxurious restaurant, but he suspected they could have had just as much fun together at her hot dog cart.

"I'll chill it," she decided. She set the bottle of wine in a plastic bucket and dumped two trays of ice cubes around it. "I like wine icy, coffee scalding—"

"And men—?" he teased lightly.

She gave him a long, appraising look and then said, "Tall, dark and handsome," with the flattering implication that he fit the description exactly.

He laughed and pulled out a dining room chair to sit on while she stirred the spaghetti sauce. "Speaking of men, and lopsided tables . . . perhaps this is none of my business, but are you still seeing that lawyer?"

She looked momentarily startled but then returned to the spaghetti sauce. "Yes, I see him occasionally. But Hugh is exactly what I told you, an old and very dear friend."

Cody hadn't any claim on her, of course, but he was glad to hear that.

The spaghetti was terrific. She also served a green salad with a spicy dressing that she'd made herself. The wine went just right with the meal, or if it didn't, neither of them was knowledgeable enough about wine to know or care. Afterward, they discussed seeing a movie but decided on a walk in the pleasant evening, instead. When they returned, she made coffee, and they sat at the sloping table to drink it and eat a dish of peach-flavored frozen yogurt.

"I really could level this table for you." Just because her lawyer-friend Hugh couldn't do it right didn't mean he couldn't.

The phone rang while he was inspecting the length of the table legs to see which one was causing the sloping wobble. Trisha went into the bare living room, where the phone was sitting on the floor, to answer it. By the time she returned, he had squares of cardboard under two legs that did the trick. It wasn't exactly an expert craftsman's solution, but it worked. The table neither slanted nor wobbled.

"Thanks. I appreciate that. But I think I'm going to buy a new table. I might as well do it now, when I have to look for new living room furniture, anyway."

"I'm a great sofa tester," he offered.

She had no snappy or teasing comeback and seemed a little distracted as she glanced vaguely into the next room. "Actually, I think I'll get a new bedroom set at the same time—"

She broke off and blushed, apparently not realizing until then that the statement had a certain suggestiveness. It was the perfect opening for some comment about his prowess at bed testing. From the flushed look on her face, he could tell she expected something like that. But he just grinned. He wasn't about to touch that line with any length pole.

Instead, he said, "I've been thinking that I might look around and see what other properties are available on the island so I can compare prices with the building you showed me. Kauai does look like a good area in which to invest, but I might be able to find something that wouldn't take as much time and expense to put in condition to rent or resell. And isn't tangled up in possible legal problems with fore-closures and liens. Would you be interested in spending some time looking around with me?"

"I'd like to, but I was away from The Pink Turtle for over a week when I attended the reunion, so it would be rather difficult for me to take more time off right now. So unless it was after business hours..."

"I'll see. In any case, the tourist brochure in my room tells me there's an evening boat ride up to a place called the Fern Grotto around here somewhere. I suppose you've done that before, but—?"

"I'd love to," she said promptly.

He said he'd check in the morning to see if space was available on a boat the following evening and then give her a call at The Pink Turtle.

He kissed her at the door, careful to hold his growing hunger for her under taut control. And had the gratifying feeling that she was doing the same.

He drove back to his room feeling that it had been a terrific evening. She'd sounded honestly regretful that she couldn't accompany him to look at properties during business hours and pleased with his suggestion about the boat ride to the Fern Grotto. So everything was going great.

Almost.

He hadn't intended to eavesdrop on her phone conversation, but he could hardly help hearing her end of it in the small apartment. At least until she carried the phone into the bedroom and shut the door. But what he'd heard was, "No, I don't know..." Pause while the other person said something. Then, "I can't. I have company right now."

He didn't need diagrams to know that a man was on the other end of the line. Not surprising, of course. Trisha was an extremely attractive woman. She undoubtedly had not been living in a manless vacuum before he arrived on the scene, and he couldn't expect her to abandon other relationships just because he'd shown up.

What bothered him was that she'd seemed so distracted when she returned from the phone call. Except for the kiss, when he was certain he'd had her full attention, her mind had been elsewhere after the call. And he could almost swear that when he looked back over his shoulder from the sidewalk that she was looking down the street as if she were expecting someone. The possibility that he was just the first shift on a two-shift night was more than a little disturbing.

# Chapter Eight

Trisha let Hugh inside as soon as his finger touched the doorbell. She could imagine what her sometimes-curious neighbors were probably thinking: *two* male visitors in one evening.

"Hugh, what in the world could be so important that you had to see me tonight?"

"Did Cody say anything about the building? Is he interested?"

"Mildly. But he wants to see what else is available and compare prices. I think he'd prefer something that didn't need so much work."

Hugh groaned in a way that would have been melodramatic if he weren't so obviously extremely upset. Just as he had sounded on the phone when he told her he had to see her, or she wouldn't have agreed to let him come over tonight.

"Hugh, what's this all about? You said you had to talk to me about something but couldn't do it on the phone. Are you ill?"

He looked terrible, his tan like a yellowish blotch clinging to his skin, his light blue eyes peering out of pale hollows. He never was a paragon of neatness, but now his clothes and hair looked as rumpled and untidy as her "condiment" artist's.

Hugh shook his head in answer to her question about illness. "Trisha, I . . . haven't been completely honest with you." He suddenly headed for a chair at her dining room table as if he might not reach it before he collapsed. He dropped his elbows to the checked tablecloth she'd used for dinner with Cody, dipped his head and ran both hands through his light brown hair.

"I told you I was in something of a financial mess and had to sell the building. But it's more than a mess. It's a black hole. And it's about to bury me." He spread his hands on the table and looked at the palms as if hoping he'd find some help there.

Trisha heated the leftover coffee and poured two cups. "Hugh, it can't be all that bad," she protested. "I know there are problems with the building. But the worst that can happen is that the lenders will foreclose and you'll lose it. Maybe you ought to just let that happen. Swallow the loss and get out."

"Swallow the loss and get out," he repeated in a hollow tone. "If only it were that simple."

He went through a brief history of how his problems had begun, as if he needed to build up to what he had to tell her. As she already knew, he'd acquired the building, a small ownership in the building, actually, given the loans that were against it, from a client in lieu of payment of a large legal bill. The client was in a huge financial mess, his wife was leaving him and he had health problems, and Hugh hadn't wanted his bill to be yet another problem for the man. Something she didn't know was that Hugh had put ownership of the building in the name of a small corporation he'd formed, Beachboy Enterprises, thinking that he might go on to acquire other properties.

He groaned again. "I saw myself as this financially independent land baron. Then I could devote myself to noble causes that *mattered* and never again have to deal with bickering neighbors or cheating mates in some messy divorce case."

"I don't see anything wrong with that," Trisha said encouragingly. "And doesn't ownership as a corporation protect you in some way?"

"That was why I did it like that. The clever lawyer," he added with almost savage sarcasm. "With all the cleverness of the hound worrying about a flea bite when he should be worrying about the dogcatcher sneaking up on him."

"So . . . ?"

"As you know, expenses for renovating the building took off like a rocket. I borrowed more money, paying an exorbitant interest rate, because it was considered a high-risk loan—"

"Hugh, are you mixed up with a loan shark, or something?" she asked, alarmed. "The kind who do very nasty things if you don't pay?"

"No. Although if I'd known any loan sharks, I might have taken that route," he admitted. "As it was, I chose a different highway to hell. When I needed still more money to keep the renovation going and make payments on the loans, as well, I borrowed from another source. Several times I borrowed from it." He took a deep, shuddering breath. "From a source that didn't know I was borrowing from it."

"I don't understand."

"I'm handling a complicated estate. Over a period of a couple of months, I've diverted some rather large sums from the estate to make payments and pay renovation expenses on the building."

"Hugh, you didn't!" Trisha said, horrified.

"Yes, I did. I thought I could get it all paid back before anyone found out. But today, everything started to collapse. The heirs have apparently become suspicious and hired a hotshot accountant. So unless I can replace the money very soon, the whole mess is going to blow up like a terrorist bomb."

"How long do you have?"

"I can stall them for a while. But no more than a few weeks at most. The second blow also came today. A finance company I considered a last resort for bailout money turned me down."

"And if this 'borrowing' from the estate does come to light?"

"Disbarment. The end of my career as a lawyer. Criminal charges. And the courts tend to take a very dim view of lawyers who dip into client funds." His voice sounded as if it came from the depths of the black hole he said was closing in on him.

Trisha was both appalled and angry. How could he have misused funds that had been entrusted to him?

Yet, she knew how. Not for greedy gain, but to dig his way out of a mess he'd gotten into by truly caring about a client's problems, by trying to help that client out of his own hole. Just as he'd cared about her and her problems. He was not a despicable or evil person; just one who had made some very bad decisions. She couldn't abandon him and let him lose not just material things but his entire career and reputation, as well.

"I have a small savings account. You can have that," she offered, figuring rapidly. "And my credit is good. I should be able to borrow—"

He reached across the table and squeezed her hand. "Thanks, Trisha. You're a sweetheart. But the only way I can possibly get out from under is to sell the building. Get rid of the damn thing. *Now.* If a buyer takes over the loans that are on the building, and I can get enough cash in addition to pay off what's missing from the estate funds..." Hope momentarily lifted his voice, but then it sank back into the pit of despair.

"Does the broker have any prospects?"

"He's sure he can sell it. Several people have expressed interest, but they all need what the broker refers to as 'creative financing,' which takes time. And I don't *have* time. So far, only one person who apparently has ready cash available to swing the deal has actually looked at it."

"Cody?" When Hugh nodded, Trisha regretfully shook her head. "I don't think he's all that interested."

"He would be if you gave him some friendly encouragement."

Trisha stiffened with surprise at what that seemed to imply.

In spite of his problems, Hugh reared back and looked mildly indignant at her misinterpretation of his suggestion. "No, I am not suggesting you rush out and offer to jump into bed with the guy if he'll buy the building. But you could show him a pleasant time here on the island. Help him see what a fantastic place it is and how smart he'd be to invest here. Talk up the building and what a great buy it is and how disappointed you'll be if you can't move The Pink Turtle into it. Let him know his buying it would make you *very* happy. Keep him so busy he won't go out looking around for some other deal. It's not as if I'm asking you to chase after some sleazeball," he added. "You really like the guy. I know you do. And if he bought the building, you'd probably see more of him, because he'd surely come around to check on his investment now and then."

"But even if I agreed to do this, *if* I agreed to it," she repeated, "what makes you think I'd have any influence with him?"

"Oh, you could influence him, all right," Hugh said, nodding wisely. "I saw that kiss at the door."

"It was just a...friendly good-night kiss," she protested.

"With both of you using up at least a month's supply of willpower to keep from tearing each other's clothes off."

That was exaggerating, of course. But more had been going on with the kiss than either she or Cody had openly acknowledged. Which was a point that Hugh apparently hadn't factored into this dangerous equation. What about her, her emotions, her involvement with a man she found pulse-poundingly attractive, a man who, in spite of the new maturity and responsibility she saw in him, might still have no more in mind than an island fling?

As he sat there waiting for her answer, Hugh never once mentioned what he had done for her in the past. How he'd helped her through a bad time both as lawyer and friend, how if it weren't for his unfaltering faith and encouragement she might still be hitting the scales at the wrong end. How he'd helped her get started with The Pink Turtle. He had too much depth of character and was too much of a gentlemen to suggest she owed him anything. But *she* thought about it, and she did owe him, and loyalty didn't leave her much choice.

"Is it really a good buy?" she demanded. "I wouldn't be trying to talk him into making an unwise investment?"

"At the price I'm offering, it's a terrific investment. It really is, Trisha. Before I started looking...elsewhere for money, I'd already put every cent I had into the renovations, and I'm going to lose all that. If I weren't trapped in this time squeeze, there'd be no problem selling to some other buyer for a much higher price. But I am trapped. So the best I can hope for is just to get out with a big financial loss and not lose my career and future, too."

"You should have gotten out while you still *had* time!" she chided almost angrily.

"I realize that now. Hindsight vision is always twenty-twenty. Unfortunately, I was apparently stumbling along with a blindfold on."

She took a stabilizing breath. "Hugh, if I do this, will you promise, promise in *blood* if I ask it, that you will never ever do anything like this again?"

He didn't offer to open a vein on the spot or make outrageous promises. He just sat there, his shoulders slumped, and looked at her with so much misery in his eyes that she knew his nod and one-word answer came from the heart. "Never."

She took a sip of the now-cold coffee. It wasn't as if she'd be doing anything reprehensible. The building would be a good, money-making investment for Cody. And it wasn't as if what Hugh asked her to do, spend time with Cody and show him the island's attractions, was exactly a repulsive undertaking. In all honesty, she could think of nothing she'd rather do than be with Cody. From a business point of view, spending so much time away from The Pink Turtle probably wasn't wise. She would also have to pay extra wages for someone to take her place there. But if it would help Hugh salvage his future, she'd manage.

"Okay, I'll do it. At least I'll do my best," she amended.

* * *

Trisha called Cody the next morning, as soon as she'd talked to a part-time clerk about putting in more hours. This time, he'd told her where he was staying.

"I've been thinking, since you're only going to be here a short time, perhaps I could take some time off from work after all."

There was only the most infinitesimal of pauses before he said, "I'm pleased to hear that."

"I thought perhaps we could drive out to Polihale Beach this afternoon. It's at the very end of the road on the west side of the island. A beautiful beach, a little different from other parts of the island, and there's usually not many people there." Actually, it was probably the most isolated spot accessible by road on the island, certainly not a place where he'd be apt to run into any property that would tempt him to buy.

"Sounds interesting, and I'd really like to do it. But I've just set up an appointment to look at a couple of properties with a real estate agent this afternoon."

Trisha quickly covered her small rush of dismay. Cody did not waste time!

"Perhaps you could cancel the appointment?"

"Why don't you just come along? Then we can also have dinner together before we take the boat ride to the Fern Grotto this evening. I did get reservations, by the way. Eight o'clock."

Trisha quickly readjusted her plans. If he was determined to look at other property, best she be there to inject some discouraging words and steer him back to Hugh's building. To give him less time to do any dangerous prowling around and discover other good buys on his own, she added, "You haven't been to The Pink Turtle yet. If you'd like to drop in this morning..."

Again that taut pause—or was it only nerves and concern about Hugh affecting her sense of time?—before he said, "I'll be there."

They were together most of the day. He showed up at The Pink Turtle about ten-thirty. He seemed a little cool and reserved at first, which puzzled her because last evening things between them had been so warm and wonderful. But as the morning passed, and she devoted an inordinate amount of flirty attention to him, he started to thaw and looked with interest at everything from the paintings on the walls to the wood sculptures and display case of her jewelry. For Melissa, he bought a cameo pendant Trisha had carved in coral, and for Debbie, a hand-carved koa wood jewelry box.

"Although she's more apt to put fishhooks or lead weights in it," he said, laughing. "I've taken her fishing a few times."

Trisha felt a little awkward about the purchases. She hadn't invited him here to entice him into buying something from her. Then she uneasily remembered that wasn't quite true. Enticing him into buying something was exactly what she had in mind. And it was a much larger and more expensive purchase than anything in her shop. Yet it was what she had to do, and she'd better get on with it.

They bought submarine sandwiches and ate lunch at the little park down the street from The Pink Turtle. On the way back to the shop, she ducked into a flower shop, telling him to wait outside.

She returned with a lei of tiny vanda orchids, and draped it around Cody's neck. "To make up for the friendly greeting you complained you didn't receive when you arrived. Sorry I'm still a little short on dancing girls," she added, teasingly referring to his complaint the first night he'd arrived at her door.

The delicacy of the orchids contrasted with his rugged masculinity, but the lovely lei suited him as well as jeans or the dress suit he'd worn to the reunion dance. He looked handsome, sexy, like some ancient pagan god masquerading in modern dress, his true identity hinted at with the donning of the lei. The goddess Pele would surely make off with him if she had a chance. Impulsively, Trisha clasped his shoulders lightly and added a brush of lips on each cheek.

He fingered the graceful lei lightly. "That's better," he agreed. He smiled. "Does this mean I'm truly welcome now?"

"Truly."

He returned the kisses she'd given him on the cheeks, the thaw complete now. With the delicious hint that he'd like to do much more than kiss her cheeks.

She kept some clothes at The Pink Turtle, and she changed into jeans and T-shirt before they went to meet the real estate agent. She had no intention of letting a real estate salesman win Cody over with a high-powered sales pitch as he and Cody crawled around in some building together while she was left outside in dress and heels.

Trisha had little idea about what might impress Cody favorably as an investment, but she could tell from his attitude after they'd seen the first property that this one was no threat. It was a somewhat run-down apartment building with obviously insufficient parking space. The next offering, comparable to what she thought Hugh's building would be once the renovation was completed, looked more appealing, even to her inexperienced eye. She was not, in fact, unfamiliar with the building.

"It's a well-built, solid building. All the second-floor offices are fully occupied, and I'm sure there'd be no problem renting the empty space on the main floor," the salesman said smoothly as he showed them around. "We get inquiries about good commercial rental space all the time."

"I wouldn't be so sure about that," Trisha whispered when the salesman went on ahead of them to open a door. "I considered leasing space here for The Pink Turtle, but way out here—?" She shook her head as if the location were as isolated as the top of Mount Waialeale. Actually, she had considered leasing here at one time. Location had nothing to do with the fact that she hadn't done it, however. The owner of a dress boutique had simply beaten her to the reasonably priced space.

"Perhaps it is a rather out-of-the-way location," Cody agreed.

"Why don't we run out to Kapaa and take another look at—" She almost called it Hugh's building but caught herself in time. She didn't like being secretive with Cody, but it was Hugh's secrets she was protecting, so she had no choice. "Look at that building where I'd like to relocate The Pink Turtle."

The salesman tried to interest them in looking at one more property, but Trisha pointedly glanced at her watch and Cody declined.

Cody drove to Hugh's building again, as Trisha had suggested. She wasn't knowledgeable about investment property, but she could point out with honest enthusiasm all the reasons she thought it would be a great place for The Pink Turtle.

"Aren't location, location and location the three things the experts say are most important in considering buying property?" She'd read that somewhere. She hoped it wasn't just some inside joke she didn't understand. "And this location couldn't be better."

Cody was still noncommittal when they left, but he was enthusiastic enough when she offered leftover spaghetti for dinner.

"See? No slanting, wobbling table," he proclaimed later as they ate together.

"My hero." With sparkling eyes she reached across the table to bring his hand to her lips and award the corded back a flirty kiss.

"Got a wall you need repaired?" he responded with interest. "A new room added on?"

"With rewards...um...commensurate with the size of the job?"

He grinned. "Whatever."

The flat-bottomed boat glided up the calm, shallow water of the Wailua River, only the small chugging of the engine breaking the silence. Trisha and Cody sat apart from the others on one of the benches lining the outer section of the boat. His arm rested on her shoulders, hand caressing her upper arm lightly.

The water was dark glass in the dusky evening light, the river's banks hidden under the glossy leaves of the hau trees gracefully dipping to brush the water. Mount Waialeale loomed in the distance, the inevitable cloak of clouds concealing its top. Trisha felt as if they were sliding dreamily into the island's past, and it wasn't difficult to believe that

back in the long-lost mists of time, no one but island royalty were allowed to enter this lovely area.

They landed at the wooden dock and hand in hand followed the walkway through the jungled growth. Above, the
sky still glowed with the pink-gold of sunset, but here it was
almost night, and torches standing along the walkway
flamed to light the way. The flickering light shone on the
long, shiny leaves of the ti plants and the paler green foliage of the kukui nut tree.

"It's said that a kukui leaf falling on someone brings
good luck," Trisha whispered. Somehow a whisper seemed
the only proper form of communication here in this al-
most-mystical place.

"What better luck could I have than I'm having right
now?" he whispered back with a smoky gleam of blue eyes.

The group stood under the overhanging ferns in the am-
phitheater-size cave of the Fern Grotto while the boat crew
strummed guitars and sang to them, and when the leader
said it was the custom to kiss after the last song, Cody's response was immediate.

It wasn't a passionate kiss, here in public. Cody didn't
mold her body against his, didn't tempt her with a seductive tease of tongue. He merely touched his lips to hers,
warm and strong, but it was a kiss filled with the powerful
promise of more to come, and Trisha felt as if she might
float right up and touch one of those ferns hanging overhead. And her heart felt almost the size of the enormous
heart-shaped leaves of the wild philodendron lining the return path to the dock.

*Careful,* she warned herself. *This is business.* The point
of all this was to persuade Cody to buy Hugh's building, *not*
to fall in love with him. And yet she could almost feel it
happening, feel herself slipping into a warm golden net of
love. . . .

The return trip was livelier with group singing and hula
dances. Two pretty girls in hula skirts and orchid leis offered to teach anyone who was interested. Trisha was no
hula expert, but she'd been inveigled into these learning
sessions before, and Cody never took his eyes off her as she
swayed hips and hands with the romantic music while less

experienced learners giggled and groaned with their awkward efforts.

On the drive home, because she knew Hugh would be calling to check on progress, she got back to business and asked, "Are you planning to look any further into buying that building in Kapaa?" She'd decided that was the safe, descriptive way to refer to it. "It's such a large, attractive building, and in such a good, busy location."

"Don't you ever think about anything but that damn building?" He sounded mildly exasperated. "Here we take a romantic boat ride and I'm thinking moonlight and kisses and you're thinking square footage and traffic count."

"Well, it is important to me. I'm anxious to move The Pink Turtle into it," she returned defensively. But his remark reminded her that she must be careful here. The idea was to gently *persuade* him to buy the building, not become an annoying nag about it. She also didn't know enough about property to appeal to his expertise as a shrewd investor. Her comments about location had pretty well exhausted her knowledge about investment property. She had to appeal to him on a more personal basis.

"If you bought it, you're already assured of one tenant." Deliberately provocative, she added with a coquettish sideways glance, "A very *congenial* tenant."

He looked across the dimly lit interior of the car at her. "How congenial?" he teased.

"I guess you won't know until you're the landlord," she returned airily.

"Actually, I've been thinking I might contact some other contractors about the cost of completing the renovations. The broker has an estimate from the contractor who's done the work so far, but I might be able to find someone who could finish the job at a lower cost."

"That sounds like a marvelous idea."

And a good place to drop the subject of the building.

Back at her door, he asked, "Would I have to make wild promises of good behavior in order to be invited in for another cup of coffee?"

Trisha tilted her head at him and with a flash of mischie-
vousness said, "Perhaps we should define 'good behavior.'"

He smiled. "I haven't noticed any oversize books of
Shakespeare around your apartment, but I've seen some
rather vicious-looking jewelry-making tools. I imagine
you'll let me know if I try to step beyond the line."

But just where would she draw the line if he came inside?
He may have accused her of thinking only of the building,
but that was far from true. The kiss at the Fern Grotto still
lingered on her lips, delicious and tingling. The feel of his
eyes following the sway of her hips as she danced the hula
for him still felt like a sweet caress that heated more than her
outer surface. Behind her, she was conscious of the empty
loneliness of the apartment, an emptiness that seductively
invited her to fill it with his warm male presence, to share
not only coffee but laughter and kisses. And perhaps not
send him away....

"Tonight," she said lightly, drawing on stern reserves of
willpower, "the line stops at my door."

He grinned and drew her into his arms, and here there was
nothing to inhibit the passion of the kiss, nothing to keep
him from welding her body against his until she felt as if
only the strength of his arms kept her from sliding into a
puddle at his feet.

His tongue circled the soft opening of her mouth, dipping inside to tease and tempt her, retreating to dance with
the delicacy of the hula against her lips. Until with a small
groan, she clamped gentle teeth against his tongue, captur-
ing it inside her mouth. One arm remained at her waist, a
steel-velvet trap holding her against the hard length of his
body, but the other hand roamed like a free spirit into
realms of angelic sweetness and wicked temptation. Fingertips found the back of her neck, and the nape that had never
been more than an uninteresting bump now felt hot and
sensitive under the sensuous circle of his caresses. He
brushed her temple and circled her ear, the gentle tug of his
fingertips on her earring reaching inside to tug something
deeper.

And then that free-spirited hand slipped down to grip her hip, palm gently turning her pelvis toward his before leaving to rise to the side of her breast and caress the soft bulge created by the crush of her breasts against his chest. The roving fingertips went farther, slipping between them to find the peak of a breast that not even the crush of their bodies could keep from turning into a hard, sensitive button.

Cody smiled when he finally lifted his mouth from hers, but his voice had a giveaway huskiness that belied the lightness of his words when he said, "That was a very lovely kiss, Miss Congenial Tenant. May I expect more at a later date?"

"Perhaps. If you're a... very congenial landlord."

"Lunch at the park tomorrow?" he asked before he let her go. "I'll bring sandwiches."

"I'm looking forward to it."

And it was a very good thing, she thought shakily after she closed the door, that she had already drawn the line at the door, because after that kiss, it was beginning to feel like a very weak and fuzzy line indeed.

She called the waiting Hugh immediately to give him a progress report. She thought Cody's plan to talk to some other contractors was encouraging, but all Hugh said was a terse, "When?"

"I don't know. He didn't say."

Hugh groaned. "He could mess around for *days* with stuff like that. And this accountant is sniffing around like a bloodhound. When are you seeing Cody again?"

"Lunch tomorrow."

"Then give him a hint that another buyer is interested, and if he doesn't act fast, he's going to miss out on a terrific deal."

Cody was waiting when she arrived at the bench in the park the following noon hour. As they ate the roast beef sandwiches he'd bought from a nearby deli, Trisha told him about having heard that another buyer was really interested in the building in Kapaa.

Repeating Hugh's words she added, "If you don't act fast, you might miss out on a terrific deal."

She set the sandwich half eaten on the bench. She did not feel at all comfortable with this. So far, although she'd withheld some facts from him, she hadn't told him anything contrary to truth. She did believe the building was an excellent buy and in a good location, and she was anxious to move The Pink Turtle into it. But this statement about another eager buyer was an outright fabrication.

"Where did you happen to hear that?" Cody asked.

That stopped her short. *Where had she happened to hear that?* "I'm not sure. Perhaps from the owner of another shop who'd like to move there also." Another lie.

"What difference would it make if someone else buys the building? I'm sure another new owner would be happy to lease space to both you and the other shop owner."

"But I want you to buy it. Then you'd have a good reason to visit Kauai often." She said it with a deliberately flirtatious smile, but this was no lie, nor was it simply a sales pitch to help Hugh. "In fact," she added, bolder yet, "I'm going to do everything I can to persuade you to buy it. I intend to show you all the wonders and delights of Kauai—"

"All?" he asked with meaningful laugh and dance of eyes.

"All the scenic delights," she corrected.

"Aw, shucks, I thought—"

"I know what you thought," she returned with spirit.

"I have lots of thoughts where you are concerned," he said, his expression unexpectedly thoughtful behind a teasing smile.

"It's scenic delights I'm offering," she repeated firmly, to make that plain to herself as well as to him.

"A beautiful guide offering a tour of scenic delights does sound appealing," he agreed. "Indeed, quite irresistible. But I could buy a different property and have just as much reason to visit Kauai."

Yes, he could, she thought with small rush of panic, because she had no quick answer for that.

But he saved her from having to answer by adding meaningfully, "Not that I need any more reason than the one I'm looking at right now."

* * *

Trisha was leaving no island delight unexplored in fulfill-
ing her promise to show him all Kauai's wonders, Cody
thought as they lay on the beach after an afternoon of surfing. They were side by side on a blanket spread on the sand,
and he rested his palm on her bare thigh. Her skin had a
golden glow in the afternoon sunlight, her hair a fresh scent
of sea and sunshine. He'd surfed a little when he was attending the university in California, but she was more skilled
than he was. He barreled along with more strength than expertise, occasionally going down in an avalanche of surf, but
she, like some graceful combination of mermaid and angel,
blithely balanced bare inches ahead of the curling lip of a
thundering wave.

In the past few days, they had hiked to hidden waterfalls, browsed in the Kauai Museum, visited the royal birth-
stones where the royalty of ancient days came to give birth
to their aristocratic offspring, sunbathed and swam at Lu-
mahai Beach, a beauty spot favored by moviemakers, and
even watched a bit of a television series being filmed there.
He'd attended a fashion show where she was modeling,
looking sophisticated and glamorous. They danced and tried
different restaurants, everything from a Polynesian feast to
magnificently messy barbecued ribs in a run-down bar that
looked as if Humphrey Bogart might stroll in any minute.

She suggested a helicopter trip, saying several outfits on
the island offered sight-seeing flights, and he'd surprised her
by renting a helicopter and piloting it himself for an evening trip. Just the two of them, hovering delicately over
Kalalau Valley, soaring up the green face of Mount Waialeale, drifting past iridescent waterfalls and over the blaz-
ing cliffs of Waimea Canyon. They saw the sun go down
over the sea in such a flaming explosion of glory that he
could see Trisha was touched to the point of happy tears.

They also talked, about everything from philosophy to
philodendrons, love to lava, dreams to disasters, and he felt
a companionship with her that was, paradoxically, both
more hotly exciting and sweetly soothing than anything he'd
known with any other woman. One time when he called

Melissa, Trisha also talked to her and Debbie briefly, and Melissa later expressed tentative approval of her.

His friend Al got in touch with him to say that the Kilauea volcano was putting on a good show, so he went over and spent a couple of days on the Big Island, reluctantly leaving Trisha behind. Al offered him a position on the research team, which he found an attractive proposition. He told Trisha about the offer when he returned to Kauai, and she was gratifyingly enthusiastic about the idea of his moving to the islands. But when he told her that he'd also looked at some commercial property on the Big Island, she was visibly upset.

"But why would it make any difference if I bought there?" he said. "It's only a couple of airplane hops away."

"It just wouldn't be the same," she said stubbornly.

That seemed vague and illogical to him, not characteristic of Trisha's usual sharp thinking. There were a couple of other things that troubled him more, however.

One evening, when leaving her apartment, he noticed the drapes on the front window weren't closed tight, and through the slit he saw her pick up the phone and start dialing before he even reached his car. Which really meant nothing, of course. She had friends. Her ex-roommate, Leslie, had joined them for lunch one day. Perhaps she and Leslie shared girl talk after a date. Although rushing to exchange midnight confidences seemed out of character with what he knew of Trisha.

Another time, after dropping Trisha off at her apartment, he'd had a flat tire on his rental car on the way back to his room. He'd been parked off to the side of the road, changing the tire, when a car zipped by. He'd almost swear it was Trisha's; he thought he'd even caught a glimpse of pale golden hair. But what would she be doing out at that time of night? Business with the The Pink Turtle? Highly unlikely. Late-night shopping trip? Doubtful. He'd briefly thought about going back to the apartment to check on her, but that had seemed like a cheap shot and he hadn't done it.

The uneasy thought that had occurred to him early on bounced into his head again, as it had several times. That maybe he wasn't the only guy in her life, that maybe she was seeing someone else, keeping late-night dates after parting with him. He'd dismissed her relationship with Hugh Lawton, because she'd seemed so sincere in her claim that he was just a friend. But that didn't mean she wasn't seeing *someone* on the sly. Someone with whom she had a more intimate relationship than she had with him ...?

He had no exclusive claim on her, of course. No right to ask her to account for hours she wasn't with him. But sometimes, he half wished he had gone back and checked on her that night.

Yet, if she was seeing someone else, it was a rather odd situation. She was always available to him. If he didn't suggest doing something together for a day or evening, she did. They were together so much, in fact, that he sometimes feared she might be neglecting her business. But when he lightly brought up that subject, she assured him she had a very competent woman handling things for her and she could catch up on her jewelry-making later.

He was also puzzled by the way she was so hung up on his purchasing that particular building in Kapaa. Actually, although he still wanted to run some figures by his accountant, he was coming to the conclusion that it was the best buy on the island and would be an excellent investment. The engineer he'd hired to inspect it had given the building good marks.

More importantly, he was coming to another inescapable conclusion. He was falling in love with Trisha. And thinking more strongly each day about making an exclusive claim on her.

If he could just get past that niggling little feeling that something was not quite right here.

# Chapter Nine

On a Monday, they went shopping together for furniture. Trisha selected a new table and chairs for her small dining area, plus a television set and living room furniture. She decided, however, to postpone buying a new bedroom set.

"Coward," Cody teased knowingly.

"I am not," she countered, controlling a tilt toward a giveaway sputter of indignation. "It's just that I've already spent a lot of money." She glanced at her watch. "And it's getting late."

"Coward," he repeated cheerfully.

Okay, she admitted to herself if not to him, *coward*. There was something simply too suggestive, too intimate, about looking for bedroom furniture with Cody. Her present bed was a chaste single, but she had room for a double now that she'd moved her workshop into the other bedroom, and she hadn't yet decided what to buy.

Inner-voice question: *So why would you need a double? You've gotten along fine with a single all this time.*

Answer: *Well, it would be much more roomy and comfortable. I do toss and turn a lot . . .*

Retort: *Ha!*

She realized Cody was watching her and laughing while she had this inner discussion with herself, which reinforced her decision. No way was she going to go around testing mattresses with Cody watching. Or, worse, with Cody making "helpful" remarks while bouncing on them with carefree abandon himself.

"I'll decide about a bedroom set later," she said firmly.

The furniture was delivered late the following afternoon. Trisha left work a little early to meet the delivery van. Actually, she'd wanted to take the whole day off, because Cody had said he had an interesting apartment building to look at, but Anne couldn't work that day, so Trisha had to be there with the less-experienced part-time clerk. She had the deliverymen place the furniture where the old pieces had been in the small room, but by the time Cody arrived that evening, she was eyeing the arrangement with dissatisfaction.

There was no choice about where the new table went, of course, and they ate dinner at it, her special Chinese concoction of a dozen different vegetables.

"But I think that table and lamp should be at the opposite end of the sofa," she decided as she looked once more through the doorway into the living room.

Cody moved table and lamp.

"Hmm." She eyed the small change critically. There was something unbalanced about it. "Perhaps the sofa would look better against this other wall. Then the television could go in that corner—"

Together they wrestled the sofa to the new location, which also meant rearranging the new love seat, coffee and end tables, television set, lamps and mirror and painting on the wall.

"That's terrible," Trisha said, dismayed with the results. "It makes the room look like the before picture in a makeover."

"You're running out of walls," Cody said.

True. Furniture couldn't be placed in the traffic pattern between living room and kitchen, which eliminated one wall. But that still left the end wall for the sofa. The room was too small for any creative away-from-the-walls arrangement.

Once more they wrestled everything to new positions. Once more the room looked awkward and unbalanced.

"Unless you're inclined to do something really unique, such as hanging the love seat from the ceiling, there's only one choice left," he observed.

Right. Move it all back the way it had been originally.

She draped her arms around his neck. "Do you mind? I'll take you out and buy you the biggest coconut and macadamia nut ice-cream cone you can find as a reward," she coaxed.

Cody had become quite addicted to that special island variety of ice cream since coming to Kauai. He had, in fact, taken to all of island life with alacrity. He even liked poi, that Hawaiian food that most newcomers labeled some version of "yukky-tasting paste." He wore brilliant aloha shirts now, the one he was wearing tonight a jungle green emblazoned with flamboyant birds of paradise. Some mainland men put on colorful Hawaiian clothes and never managed to look anything but awkward and foolish, but the shirts only emphasized Cody's athletic body and irresistible flash of smile and dance of eyes.

"I can think of a more interesting reward." He grinned like a dark pirate bargaining for the prettiest captive.

"You have an overactive imagination," she chided as severely as one could chide a wickedly handsome pirate in an aloha shirt.

"Imagination," he declared with the air of one deeply wounded, "appears to be *all* I have." Then he gave an exaggerated sigh. "But, as my niece Debbie says, life is tough."

"Very tough," Trisha agreed without sympathy.

They rearranged the furniture once more, the final arrangement encompassing only a switch between wall positions of mirror and a painting of a clown. They went out for the promised ice cream, Trisha eating a moderate scoop, Cody an oversize double. When they returned to the apartment, he looked over her shoulder into the newly furnished room.

"I'm really worn-out from all that furniture moving." He emphasized tiredness with a big yawn. "Maybe I could just sleep on your new sofa tonight so I wouldn't have to drive all the way back to my room?''

If she believed Cody had in mind sleeping on the sofa, she could qualify as Miss Naive of the Year. But she couldn't really be angry with him. Teasingly she said, "You make the five-mile drive sound like a swim to the mainland."

"You haven't lived until you've tasted my scrambled eggs," he coaxed.

"If you'd like to come in and fix some right now..."

"I'm full of ice cream now. But I could make some for breakfast, and perhaps add a croissant or two...." His dark eyes glinted with mischief, but she knew he was serious enough about wanting to stay the night.

It had been obvious for some time that he would like to carry their relationship to a more intimate level, but, as always, he was patient and good-humored and teasing rather than pushy or unpleasant about it. She had to admit thoughts about a deeper intimacy also strayed into her mind with increasing frequency, and when he kissed her, it was a hungry desire threatening to explode out of control.

So why not do it? She wouldn't even have to say anything, just open the door wide and their healthy man-woman desires would take over.

She wasn't totally certain why she didn't do it. Maybe because she still saw a dangerous potential for heartbreak here. He was sweet and exciting, fun and affectionate, companionable, dynamic, intelligent, a man who appealed to her with a hot depth of sexuality she'd never before known. If she'd had to make a list of the qualities she could want in a man, he had them all. Except for one small thing. There was that tiny bit of detached reserve she sometimes sensed in him, a small drawing back that warned her that her emotional feelings for him were perhaps leaping ahead of his for her. There was also the tenuousness of the future. Even if he bought Hugh's building, she knew he intended to leave it in the hands of a manager, that his presence on the island wasn't required.

And maybe part of her reluctance to initiate a more intimate relationship with Cody was because a certain guilt gnawed at her, a feeling that before she took this irrevers-

ible step, everything must be open and honest and above-
board between them. Which it couldn't be when Hugh's
secrets lay between them, when Hugh's secrets had become
*her* secrets. She had started this relationship with Cody on
the shaky foundation of an ulterior motive, and even though
her growing feelings for him . . . love, she suspected, if she
dared look deeply enough . . . were much different now, she
still felt uneasy about the deceit built into the situation.

"Very well," he said on a sigh when the silence stretched
out. "You'll just have to do without the most magnificent
scrambled eggs you've ever tasted for another day."

Trisha made one more change in the living room after
Cody was gone. She moved the teddy bear out of his hum-
ble position in the bedroom to a place of honor on the arm
of the love seat. He looked right at home there. More smug
than sad, as if he'd always known she would capitulate
eventually.

When Hugh's phone call for a progress report got her out
of bed an hour later, she had to admit she'd forgotten to ask
Cody what he thought about the apartment building he'd
looked at that day.

"I'm sorry," she apologized. She knew how vital this was
to Hugh, and yet she'd gotten all involved with the frivolous business of furniture. "I'll find out as soon as I can."

"Time is running out." He sounded more despondent
than desperate, as if he was almost resigned to his fate.

And it wasn't right that he lose everything over this one
mistake, enormous as it was. He'd just won an age
discrimination case, not a case of landmark importance but
a difficult one and vital to the older woman who had been
discriminated against. It was the kind of case he loved to
take on, the kind that also paid more in satisfaction of jus-
tice done than in big fees. The win had buoyed his spirits
briefly, but then he'd lost his girlfriend, Nan, who'd unexpectedly decided to go back to her former husband. He'd
sounded so desperate the night that happened that Trisha
had dropped the phone and rushed over to his condo immediately, not more than five minutes after Cody left her
apartment. She didn't think Hugh would ever get to the
point of being suicidal, but she wasn't positive. That night,

she'd stayed with him for several hours, both talking to him and encouraging him to talk, not leaving until she was certain he was in a more stable condition.

"What kind of prices are on the places he's looking at?" Hugh asked. "I've cut mine almost to the bone, but maybe I could persuade the broker to let me pay his commission in installments and get the price down a little farther yet."

"I don't always know the prices on the properties that interest him, but those I do know are comparable to yours. Some are higher. Actually, he hasn't had time to look at many. I've kept him very busy."

"Good girl."

"It's just that he's very levelheaded and prudent about making a big investment. He said a few days ago that he was having his accountant go over some figures on your building and also look into how purchase of it would affect his tax position."

"Smart guy," Hugh said wryly. "Would that I had been so smart and efficient."

"You just got a little out of your field of expertise." Hugh was being hard enough on himself; he didn't need her to come down on him, too.

Actually, Trisha was rather astonished at the price range Cody was considering in properties. Where could he possibly have gotten that kind of money? She knew he'd made a good profit on the apartment complex in Vancouver, but even so, he hadn't bought that property with the contents of some piggy bank. Yet, she'd never felt she had any right to pry, and he hadn't volunteered any information.

"Well, hang in there," Hugh said, sounding as if he expected a noose to close around his own neck any moment. "Let me know if you hear anything."

A few mornings later, Cody arrived to take her on a hike on the Na Pali trail, an outing they'd been planning for several days. He was wearing khaki shorts and an aloha shirt of brilliant red splashed with white flowers. Somewhere he'd also acquired a battered straw hat, complete with rakish black feather. He wore the hat beach-bum style, dipped low on his forehead, and he looked carefree and deliciously sexy. He also had a gift for her.

"I bought it because it reminded me of you," he said. "The lady at the shop called it a sea angel."

The little winged "angel" was made of various sizes and shapes of seashells fastened together, one round shell painted as a face with sweetly curved mouth and long, sweeping eyelashes. The finespun, silky "hair" was a pale golden color, indeed much like Trisha's.

"See? It even has a little golden halo," he said. He laughed, eyes rich with familiar teasing lights. "That *really* reminded me of you."

The little angel gently made fun of Trisha's reluctance to take the big step into intimacy with him, but it was also a sweet and delightful gift, one she knew she'd long treasure. She set it on the end table by the love seat, right next to the teddy bear.

He reached up and pretended to check the position of an invisible halo hovering over her own head. "Yep, still there," he said, and sighed.

Oh, but slipping, she thought, both tremulous and smiling. Tilting, drooping, sliding...

Yet, at the same time, the small gift gave her an uncomfortable twinge of guilt. There was something so sweetly innocent about it. Cody thought *she* was sweetly innocent. Yet she was hardly any innocent angel with the deceptive scheme she was working on.

She picked up her backpack containing their lunch, a large tube of SPF 15 sun cream and a plastic container of water. She was in hiking shoes, plus denim shorts and a white crop top that revealed a flash of slim midsection. She added sunglasses and a white eyeshade, bringing the long braid that started high on the back of her head up through the open top of the eyeshade, where it swung like a flirty filly's tail. As they walked to the car, Cody picked a luscious red hibiscus that matched the ribbon on her braid and stuck it in the band of her cap, grinning at her as if he thought she was also luscious.

They drove north, passing Hugh's building in Kapaa along the way. On such a glorious day, Trisha didn't really want to think, much less discuss what she was beginning to think of, as Cody had once referred to it, "that damn building." But an older couple was standing by a car in the parking lot and it was too good an opportunity to let pass.

"Oh, look, I wonder if that's someone considering purchasing the building?" She doubted it was; the couple had *tourists* written all over them. But their presence made a good opening for a casual question. "Have you received any comments on the figures you supplied your accountant?"

"He thought they looked good, although he suggested the projected rental rates per square foot were perhaps a little low."

Trisha had told him the price Hugh had been going to charge her for space for The Pink Turtle. Which she was reasonably certain *was* a little low; Hugh wasn't one to drive a hard bargain. "I'd be willing to pay more than I'd originally planned," she said quickly, also taking the opportunity to throw in another sales blurb for the building. "It's such a desirable space."

"No business talk today, okay?" he said. He didn't sound annoyed, just firm. "Today is just for fun."

They drove past cane fields and pastures, although new houses and businesses were making inroads on the rural beauty that had helped give Kauai the name of the "Garden Island." Beyond Princeville and the incredible beauty of Hanalei Bay loomed a steep, green ridge slanting directly to the sea, the beginning of the spectacular Na Pali coast. Near the golden sands and wild surf of Ke'e Beach the road ended and the trail began, eleven rough, treacherous, up-and-down miles to the Kalalau Valley.

Trisha and Cody were not planning to hike the entire distance this day. The round-trip to the end of the trail was so strenuous that it was at least an overnight hiking trip. Their destination was Hanakoa, some six miles away. Trisha had never been there, but Hugh had told her it was away from the sea, a lovely jungled area with camping spots and a wonderful natural swimming hole.

Cody insisted on carrying the backpack. "You made the lunch. I'll carry it." He set her braid to swinging with the teasing snap of a finger. "Ready?"

"Ready."

The rough trail was not conducive to conversation. It started with a steep climb up a muddy pathway crisscrossed with treacherous roots and booby-trapped with sharp rocks. Ropy, big-leaved vines climbed the thick jungle of trees, with here and there a brilliant flash of flower or bird. Once, Trisha slipped on a steep section of slick mud and plunged rump-first into Cody who was following closely behind.

"Not a trail for the out-of-shape," Cody commented. He'd managed to catch her and keep them both upright. He grinned. "Your shape, however, feels just fine."

"This is the easy part."

"I'm not complaining." He kissed her on the back of the neck and then gave her a little push on the bottom to get her going again, apparently enjoying this fringe benefit of the hike.

About twenty minutes of climbing brought them to a wind-ripped point with a panoramic view of sea and surf and mountains. Row after row of incredibly green ridges sloped steeply to meet the raging surf, like the exposed backs of sharp-spined dinosaurs slumbering since some prehistoric age of giants. Close to shore, the water was a pale green; farther out, it shaded to blue and royal purple. A helicopter flew past, so close they could see the passengers waving, the sound of the engine an intrusion even over the roar of surf.

Two miles of hiking brought them to lovely Hanakapiai Beach, but they rested only briefly before going on.

Beyond Hanakapiai, the trail grew ever rougher, sometimes so narrow only an overhead ribbon of blue sky showed between rough walls of jungled growth. Trisha, tilting her head back to look up, found it almost disorienting, as if she was looking down into a strip of serene blue water. But in this raw, wild area, real water was not serene. In places the trail dipped so low that cold spray from surf crashing over the rock ledges spattered her skin, and in others it rose to perch precariously on the edges of windswept cliffs plunging straight to the surf, where far below an excursion raft looked like a colorful toy tossed by the sea. They met one couple with camping gear hiking out, but other than that, the wild beauty of the trail was theirs alone, their own private Eden.

As the trail drifted away from the sea to climb to Hanakoa, Trisha turned her head to say something to Cody about stopping for a snack. It was the wrong time to take her eyes off the trail. Her foot caught on something, rock or exposed root, and she tumbled forward, ignominiously landing facedown and rump up in a shallow green ravine beside the trail.

Cody scrambled down to help her to her feet. "Are you okay?"

"I think so. Other than being embarrassed by my own clumsiness." She'd also lost her white eyeshade and the red ribbon on her braid. He retrieved both, but she just stuck the ribbon in her pocket and let her hair fall loose.

She wasn't totally okay, however, she realized when she climbed back up to the trail. She'd apparently twisted her ankle slightly, nothing serious or incapacitating, but she could feel enough of a twinge to let her know she'd better head back rather than continuing farther on the trail.

"I'm really sorry. I'll wait here for you if you want to keep going."

Cody shook his head. "We'll do it another time." He grinned, ever the optimistic opportunist. "Maybe next time we'll make it an overnight camping trip together."

They snacked on an orange each while Trisha rested her ankle, and then made their way at a slower pace back to the beach at the edge of a small bay nestled like a rough jewel at the bottom of a green valley. They took off their shoes and sat cross-legged in the shade at the edge of the crescent of sand, and both launched into the ham-and-tomato sandwiches, baked beans, coleslaw and more oranges as if they hadn't eaten in a week.

"How's the ankle?" Cody asked when they were through eating and Trisha was gathering every scrap of plastic and peel so as to leave nothing of their presence in this idyllic place.

She wiggled her foot. "Getting better."

"Good. We're in no rush. We'll just give it some more time to rest before we start back." He spread his shirt in the sun on the sand and stretched out on his stomach.

"It's easier to get a burn here than you might realize," Trisha warned. With her fair coloring she always had to be careful, but even someone with a tan like Cody's could sometimes get an unexpected burn under the potent Hawaiian sun.

"Then how about breaking out some of that sun cream you brought along?"

Trisha uncapped the tube and knelt beside him to dribble a squiggle of cream on his left shoulder blade. It instantly fell into a curved shape, like a letter of the alphabet. A *C* for Cody? Or maybe it was an *L*. An *L* for love. . . .

Briskly she discarded that line of thought and added another swirl of cream on the other shoulder. With her palms she spread both squiggles over the tanned skin, warm from both exertion and sun. The smooth muscles under her hand were relaxed but not soft, long muscles running along his spine, thicker bunches of muscles massed between neck and shoulder. The entire anatomy of his back was open to her hands and eyes, but even with his body relaxed and eyes closed there was nothing defenseless about him. Taking a sensuous joy in the practical excuse for full exploration, she spread the cream with short strokes along the slant of his shoulder blades, long strokes from the line of dark hair curling softly against his neck, down the solid ridge of his spine to the point where it curved to an indentation and disappeared into his khaki shorts. She did the sides of his ribs and the backs of his arms. She even did the backs of his ears, drawing a fingertip along the soft, sensuous curves. She felt a reaction in him, a little ripple, as if that touch went beyond the skin to something deeper and even more sensitive.

"Ears are very important," she said, feeling a small necessity to defend that action. "They burn more easily than people realize." They were also delightful to explore.

"I thank you," Cody murmured from the depths of his crossed arms where his head lay. "My ears thank you."

Growing ever bolder, she moved down to the backs of his legs, hard with muscle, rough with dark masculine hair. She had the strangest urge to kiss him right on the hard cord at the back of his ankle, a place that had never before even remotely interested her in any man. But then, everything about Cody interested and appealed to her....

Hastily returning to the expanse of his back, before she gave in to that unlikely temptation, she swirled extravagant patterns of curlicues and circles and flowing X's with her moving palms.

"What are you doing?" Cody inquired mildly. "It feels as if you're drawing pictures or writing secret messages. Not that it doesn't feel *good*, mind you."

Were her hands subconsciously writing secret messages on his bare skin? She stopped for a moment, only her fingertips touching warm muscles. *Trisha loves Cody?* Or perhaps the hands were receiving secret messages. *Cody loves Trisha.* If only that was true....

"Okay, if you're so clever, what does the message say?" she challenged.

He lay motionless for a moment while she rubbed his back in nonmessage swirls.

"I get it. It's clearly saying, Cody, turn over—" he rolled over on his back, grin teasing and mischievous "—and kiss me."

He pulled her down on top of him, trapping her long, bare legs with his. The skin exposed at her midriff by her crop top met his bare midsection and welded to it, feminine honey gold against male bronze. Her hair fell like a rippling curtain around them, creating a gold-tinted world occupied only by their two faces. Her eyes were just above his, each detail of his features in magnified close-up. The heavy slash of dark eyebrows, the beginnings of little sun crinkles at the corners of his eyes. Eyes so blue that not even the color of the turbulent sea could compete, eyes that were laughing at her, teasing her, tempting her. Nose that wasn't as perfectly straight as she'd always thought it was. She ran a fingertip down it, pausing on the almost invisible slant to one side.

"Motorcycle accident," he said wryly. "Which also knocked out my two front teeth. How do you feel about a guy with two phony front teeth?"

What she felt was an odd tenderness toward those two front teeth. The fact that they were "phonies" gave him an unexpected vulnerability that hadn't been there before. Deliberately she dipped her head and touched the tip of her tongue to them. He groaned and with tender roughness captured the tongue between his teeth.

And then her eyes drifted shut, and her other senses took over. She felt the strength of his mouth and tease of his tongue, heard a thundering rumble and didn't know if it was surf or her heartbeat; tasted the fresh sweetness of his mouth, still faintly flavored with orange. She felt his hands slip beneath the back of her short blouse and caress her skin, lightly at first and then with deepening hunger. He rearranged the fabric of the blouse so that only the spiderweb lace of her bra separated her breasts from the heat of his chest, and his hands roamed lower, stroking the curve of her denim-clad bottom.

She lifted her head, and in one swift movement he reversed their positions so that her back was against his shirt on the sand, warm and a little damp with his sweat. He kissed her mouth and arched throat, then shifted his weight to one side and dipped his lips to her bare midriff and drew circles with his tongue on skin that seemed to shiver with delight under the touch. Then she was beneath the virile strength of his body, the shadow of his head covering her closed eyes, and the indistinct yearnings within her coalesced into focused desires.

"Trisha?" he whispered, the movement of his lips brushing hers as he spoke the electric word.

Trisha didn't have to ask what the one softly whispered word meant. They were alone in their own private world of sun, sand and surf, and her body and heart blazed with desire. And something even more important blazed like a headline across her mind. *I love you, Cody Malone,* it said, an admission that she could hold back no longer. Her eyes met his, and her hands crossed behind his neck and her body arched with taut eagerness.

But something moved into the peripheral edge of her vision, a flicker of sunlight on metal, and a moment later her ears separated the whir of helicopter blades from the roar of surf. As usual, the helicopter was flying low enough that she could distinguish outlines of both pilot and passengers. The craft came to a stop, hovering overhead, more inquisitive insect than hummingbird. And the passenger in the front seat had a video camera aimed directly at the two of them!

Trisha squirmed out from under Cody and scrambled to a sitting position, trying to straighten her hair and yank her blouse down all at once. They were, she realized in embarrassed dismay, the starring actors in someone's home video, their moment of intimacy on display as a tourist souvenir of Hawaii. And if the helicopter had arrived only a few moments later, it might well have been an x-rated video.

The helicopter pilot, apparently deciding the fun was over, waved and turned the whirring craft in a smooth, upward arc, and a moment later it disappeared over a green ridge.

An aura of heat and desire still shimmered between them, but the moment of rapidly blooming intimacy was definitely over.

"We should be going," Trisha said awkwardly.

Cody picked up his beach-bum hat and slammed it on his head. For a moment, anger and frustration snapped in his eyes. But then he shook his head and grinned. "Shot down by a video camera," he muttered ruefully.

Trisha couldn't help but giggle, and then they were both laughing, giggles and chuckles rising to helpless spasms of laughter. She laughed with a strange mixture of relief, her own frustration, the ridiculousness of the situation... and love. She didn't know for certain why he laughed, but she loved him all the more for being the kind of man who could lose anger and frustration in laughter with her.

When they hiked back to the car, they were as companionable as ever, but when they stopped to rest, their eyes met and then they were laughing again.

\*   \*   \*

She had to do something about this situation. She was becoming more and more uncomfortable with the game of deceit she was playing.

She talked to Hugh on the phone about it that very night, suggesting that they simply take Cody into their confidence and tell him why it was so important that he buy that building.

"You're in love with him, aren't you?" Hugh asked.

"Yes." She still felt a little foolish being caught in such an incriminating position by a quick-triggered tourist with a video camera, but it didn't change the fierce knowledge that had come to her. Yes, she loved him. She smiled to herself as she thought of his confession about the two front teeth. She loved those phony front teeth, too, along with everything else about him. But this secret that lay between them felt like sandpaper on her heart.

"He's in love with you?"

"I'm ... not sure."

She knew he found her desirable and attractive, that he enjoyed being with her. She was reasonably certain now that she wasn't just an island fling; several times she was almost certain the words *I love you* had hovered on his lips. But they had never been spoken.

Hugh's response didn't surprise her. "Trisha, I can't keep you from telling him, but I'm asking you not to. You can't know for certain what he might do with the information if he had it. And once he does have it, then it's too late."

Love for Cody...loyalty to Hugh. Trisha felt trapped. But Hugh was right. She had no idea what Cody might do with such incriminating information. Just as she didn't know for certain the true depth of his feelings for her.

"Just keep working on him, please?" Hugh asked. "You'll be doing him a favor in making a fine investment. And you'll be saving my ... skin."

She knew he'd started to say "life" and changed it to the less desperate word. She took a steadying breath. "Okay, I'll do my best."

"When are you seeing him again?"

"At noon tomorrow. If I'm working, we always meet at that little park near The Pink Turtle for lunch. And we're going to a luau later this week."

"I hope things work out for you and Cody. You deserve happiness, Trisha, lots of it. This should all be over soon."

Right. One way or the other, it would soon be over. It was just a question of whether Cody's money or that bloodhound accountant got to Hugh first.

# Chapter Ten

The luau was at the home of the real estate broker handling the building Trisha was always trying to convince him, sometimes subtly, sometimes not so subtly, he should buy. Actually, Cody liked to tease her about it a bit, because she ruffled so easily on that subject. The teasing was about to come to an end, although he was undecided whether to tell her tonight or wait until the transaction was accomplished.

The spectacular two-story cedar house, with vaulted ceilings and wide decks, sat on a bluff overlooking an equally spectacular view of a secluded cove fringed with ironwood. The lower deck swirled with color, the women's dresses, the men's casual shirts and the wild profusion of potted plants. It was Trisha from whom Cody could hardly remove his eyes, however.

Her hair was the way he liked it best, like a pale golden waterfall around her shoulders, and she'd clipped a fragrant white flower behind her ear. Her earrings were small and simple, iridescent blue squares of abalone shell. She wore a *pareau*. This night, she had wrapped it to leave one tempting shoulder bare, and it was all he could do to keep from raining a continuing shower of kisses on that shoulder. The shimmery turquoise-and-white fabric clung to the graceful curves of her body in a way that aroused conflicting desires. One was simply to stand off and admire her; the other was to slowly start peeling it away until she was naked in his arms.

Once, she'd laughingly said to him when he'd whispered some sweet nothing in her ear as they danced barefoot in the sand, "Cody Malone, I'll bet you could *charm* your volcanoes into submission or eruption."

But could he do that to *her?*

Their host made a few introductions and then left them on their own. Cody had earlier had the impression Trisha wasn't eager to attend this luau, but as they circulated, she seemed poised and at ease. She knew some of the people, mostly from having met them through The Pink Turtle, he gathered. One woman touched the long, dramatic black earrings on her own ears and smiled when she said, "My favorites," and he knew they were Trisha's design. Tantalizing scents of roasting meat joined with the exotic scents of flowers and expensive perfumes. Cody, like most of the men, was dressed in white pants and bright shirt, although this one, with dark blue dolphins cavorting on a pale blue background, was less flamboyant than some he'd acquired on the island.

He did sneak a couple of kisses onto that creamy shoulder when they joined the line winding past the redwood tables loaded with food. Succulent roast pig from an underground pit, *lomilomi* salmon, teriyaki chicken, poi, rice, noodles, egg rolls, a dozen different salads, fresh pineapple, coconut pudding and his favorite ice cream, coconut and macadamia nut. An elaborate stereo system supplied romantic guitar music.

After the meal, their host, the real estate broker, bore down on them with a purposeful expression that Cody knew meant he planned to get down to what this luau was really all about—promoting business. Cody didn't need to hear any more praise of that building in Kapaa, however. He'd already made up his mind.

"Terrific luau," he said. He turned Trisha away with a hand on her elbow. "We've just decided to take the trail down to your beautiful beach."

"Fine! Enjoy yourselves. Maybe we can get together later."

"Do you mind?" he whispered as he guided Trisha toward the dozen redwood steps that led down to the trail. She was in white heels, not the ideal footwear for trail walking.

"Nothing I'd like better."

She promptly reached down and slipped off the white sandals. And the fact that she was the kind of woman who could do that was another of the many reasons he knew he was falling in love with her. He also loved the fact that she could be at home in something so femininely frivolous as the high-heeled sandals and yet be equally at home skimming the wild waves on a surfboard. He led the way down the trail, turning to offer her a hand occasionally in the steeper places. And a couple of times, he stopped solely to kiss that irresistible shoulder. At the end of the trail, they had the small cove to themselves, the gentle surf writing silver scrolls against the sand.

Cody put his arms around her and kissed her thoroughly on the mouth. "There," he said with satisfaction. "It's been much too long since I did that."

Trisha laughed. "All of... what? Two hours?" He loved that laugh, too, whether it was giggle or chuckle or outright guffaw.

"Much too long," he repeated. He made a sudden decision. This wasn't anything he'd planned for tonight, but here, in this serene and lovely cove, the time seemed right. He braced himself lightly, because this was never an easy subject for him, and said, "Let's sit down. I want to talk to you."

He was holding her by both hands, and he felt a quick dampness rise to her palms, as if she was suddenly apprehensive.

"Nothing terrible," he assured her.

She didn't look convinced. She sat on the sand with her feet tucked under her, expression faintly wary. He stretched out on his side beside her, body supported with an elbow propped in the sand.

"How do you see me, Trisha?"

"I'm not sure what you mean."

"Do you still see me as the shallow guy who did you wrong back in high school?"

"No. I know you've changed."

He had placed her sandals on the sand between them, and he toyed absentmindedly with a slender white strap. "I don't suppose you knew much about me outside the school scene when we were in high school."

"I rode my bicycle past your house rather frequently." With a wry smile she added, "It was only about three miles out of my way."

He smiled, too, but he was looking into the past when he went on. "My mother was dead, as you know, and there was just the three of us, Dad, David and me. In many ways, Dad was more buddy than father, not strong on discipline, so David and I... Well, mostly me," he amended, "pretty much ran wild. Dad was always changing jobs and having checks bounce, being threatened with foreclosure on the house or repossession of his car. He liked to party and have a good time. Lots of people thought of him as irresponsible, I suppose."

He glanced up, but she was just looking at him with lips slightly parted, as if this was not at all what she'd expected to hear.

"But there was one thing about which he was responsible. He had this almost fanatic determination that if anything happened to him, there should be something for David and me. So even if we were eating pork and beans out of a can, he paid his damned life insurance." He felt a surge of the old anger that had driven him for months after the accident. An unfair and irrelevant anger, of course. *Not* having insurance wouldn't have kept his father and David alive.

"And?"

"The spring after I graduated, just a couple months before David was to graduate, the three of us went cross-country skiing in Colorado. Dad was selling real estate then, and he'd just earned some big commission and was blowing it. He called the trip David's last bachelor fling, because David and Melissa were getting married in June. I thought David was crazy to be marrying so young," Cody admitted, "but he was never like me. I think he'd been in love with Melissa since about seventh grade."

He swallowed, realized he had her hand in a death grip and purposely forced his fingers to loosen their hold.

"You already know Dad and David were killed in an avalanche on that skiing trip. I was hit by it, too." For a few minutes, the claustrophobic terror of being trapped under the snow engulfed him again. But the terror that came next was even greater. "But I was right on the edge of it, and I dug my way out. Then I started digging and trying to find them. And I couldn't. I never could. I dug and dug..." He looked down at his hands, briefly seeing them as they had been then, raw and bleeding. "And then I ran for help, and people came and dug some more. Until finally they were found, a hundred feet farther down the slope, buried under twelve feet of snow."

"Oh, Cody...Cody..." She took his hand and pressed it against her cheek and then to her lips. Tears trickled down her cheeks, but she seemed unaware of them.

"The insurance policy Dad had been paying on was a big one. Doubled in case of accidental death. And, because David was also dead, it all came to me. I hated the money," he added with a fierce vehemence after he controlled the spasm of pain in his throat. "I *hated* it."

"I can understand that."

"I left Horton, and for a while I went wild, doing every crazy, dangerous thing I could think of, as if daring fate to take me, too. Then I had the motorcycle accident. I broke my nose and several bones and lost those teeth and spent a month in the hospital. But in the same way that your accident made you step back and think, mine did, too. I took a hard look at myself and the pointless, irresponsible life I was living. Out of that came the realization that I was letting them down, Dad and David, and I decided to change."

"So you borrowed your brother's dream and became a volcanologist." She hesitated a moment. "Do you regret that? Was it a mistake?"

"No, no mistake," he said firmly. "I kept out enough money to go to college and stuck the rest in some southern

California property. Mostly I just wanted to be rid of it. It felt...bloodstained.''

Trisha nodded as if she also understood that.

He smiled wryly. ''I suppose if I'd *wanted* to make more money, I'd have lost every cent. But I really didn't give a damn, so it just multiplied like a bad virus. Some company building a mall came along a few months later and gave me more than double what I'd paid for the property. I put that into a couple more pieces of real estate and it grew again. And still it felt bloodstained.''

She rubbed his hands as if they were cold.

''And then something happened that made me see things differently. I'd just shoved Dad's and David's things into storage when I left Horton, but finally I had to return and go through them. I found a letter David had written to Melissa, apparently intending to give it to her on their wedding night. I decided she deserved to have it. But she'd left Horton, too, and it took me months to find her. When I finally did find her, she was living in Vancouver, struggling to raise Debbie alone on a waitress's earnings. Debbie was four years old before I even knew she existed. And David never knew, of course. Melissa hadn't even realized she was pregnant when he was killed.''

''Sometimes life just doesn't seem...fair.'' Trisha's throat moved in an emotional swallow in the moonlight, and he raised up and kissed her lightly on her tear-streaked cheek.

He'd showed her Debbie's photo before, but he pulled out his wallet and they looked at it together again. The photo shone in the moonlight like a glossy jewel, a little girl with dark hair and sweet smile that looked so much like David's that it brought him both pain and pleasure to look at it. He'd like to have a little Debbie of his own one of these days.

''And now the money is just money. I can see it for what it is, the result of my father's love and dedication, what he *wanted* for me. I can feel pleased instead of guilty when I make a profitable investment. Which I've been fortunate enough to do fairly consistently. There's a trust fund for Debbie so she'll be able to do whatever she wants with her future. And I've shared with Melissa, too, of course, and helped her with investments of her own."

Trisha put his hand to her cheek again, and she was smiling even though tears were still running down her cheeks. And in that moment, those lingering doubts and reservations evaporated, vanishing with them the nagging little feeling that something wasn't quite right. What he felt was no "falling" in love; he was *there*. A marrying kind of love. He could go ahead and ask her right now—

No. That wouldn't be fair. She was in an emotional turmoil now, vulnerable. When she gave him her answer, he wanted it to come from every part of her, mind, heart, body and soul. And tomorrow he'd have a ring to go with the proposal.

He would, in fact, have one, two, *three*, surprises for her!

Back in her apartment, Trisha dropped to the new love seat. Cody hadn't hinted at coming in for more than a late-night cup of coffee this evening; he had simply kissed her at the door, smiled and said, "See you at the park tomorrow?"

She absentmindedly picked up the teddy bear and traced the beady black eyes with a forefinger. She'd been reluctant to attend the luau at the home of the real estate broker handling Hugh's building, afraid that somehow something incriminating might come up. And when Cody had said he wanted to talk to her, she'd briefly panicked, certain that he was about to tell her he knew something or that he was simply going back to the mainland. That it had been fun ... thanks a lot ... see you at the twentieth reunion.

And then to find out that he had also been trapped in the avalanche and how he'd acquired the money and how he felt about it, the effort he'd put into finding Melissa and Debbie and his generosity with them.

She'd known he'd changed, but only now did she fully realize the painful depths of that change. And the depths of her love.

At midmorning the next day, she had to go to the bank for a few minutes, and when she returned Anne said Hugh had called and wanted her to call him within the next half hour, because he had to be in court the remainder of the day. She didn't do it, however. She knew what Hugh wanted. Another progress report. She hadn't called him the previous night because she was too full of the emotions of the evening. And Hugh must know by now that she'd have contacted him *instantly* if there was anything to report. She wasn't exactly annoyed with Hugh. She knew what he was going through. But she just didn't feel up to talking to him right now. She had something else on her mind.

Was there any way she could tell Cody something that would erase this deceit that shadowed their relationship...and yet not betray or jeopardize Hugh? Cody had been so open and honest in everything he'd told her last night, open and honest not only with the facts but also with his raw emotions. The fact that she had been considerably less than open and honest with him was feeling like a heavier burden by the minute.

Would it matter to him that she'd gone into their relationship with the ulterior motive of persuading him to buy Hugh's building? Foolish question. If she didn't think it would matter, she wouldn't feel so uneasy about telling him. But, of course, she *couldn't* tell him everything without the possibility of endangering Hugh. And it was still desperately important that Cody buy Hugh's building....

She had a light headache by the time she reached the park bench for lunch with Cody. She was almost glad he wasn't already waiting for her with sandwiches and soft drinks in hand, as he usually was. It gave her a little time to wrestle with her problem without the distraction of customers and business.

After fifteen minutes, however, she started to become concerned. He'd never been late before; it wasn't at all like him. After a half hour, she left the bench and uneasily circled the small park. After fifty-five minutes, when she had to return to work, it was obvious Cody wasn't coming.

Logic told her he'd simply been held up by some mundane delay, but she couldn't help worrying through a scary list of possible disasters. She felt quick relief when she walked in the door of The Pink Turtle and Anne immediately said, "Cody called." No doomsday disasters, after all.

It was a relief that disappeared as quickly as blue sky in a storm.

Cody's message was simply that he was going over to the Big Island. No explanation or apology for missing lunch, no reason for another trip to the other island, nothing about when he'd return.

How very odd. How unlike him, he who had impressed her with his utter *dependability* these last weeks. And he'd called on her lunch hour, when he knew she wouldn't be there....

With a peculiar sense of panic, she dialed the small resort hotel where he'd been staying. On his previous trip to the Big Island, he'd kept the room even though he was away for a few days.

That was not the case this time. Cody Malone had checked out.

She spent the next few minutes on a mental and emotional roller-coaster ride. At the top of the upward swoop, she assured herself that everything was fine; perhaps his friend Al had contacted him to say the Kilauea volcano was putting on another fire-and-brimstone show. At the bottom, she raged that he was simply the irresponsible, shallow guy he'd been back at Horton High. All his claims and appearances of maturity were merely an elaborate act to entice her into his bed, well-rehearsed scenes in an often-used seduction script. And when the script hadn't led where he expected, he'd tired of the game and simply...checked out.

No. She couldn't believe that. Not when she loved him the way she did.

It took her all of another fifteen minutes to make a rash and reckless decision. If he'd simply gone to visit Al again, her unexpected appearance would only please him. He'd be delighted to take her to see close up the workings of the volcano. If that wasn't the case, and he *had* walked out, her sudden appearance could be a humiliating disaster for her. But she didn't care. She would *not* let it end like this, in unexplained silence.

She was on one of the frequent, island-hopping flights within an hour. As she boarded, the thought occurred to her that this impulsive flight was not exactly rooted in solid planning, because she had no idea how to contact his friend's research team on the island. By the time the plane landed, however, she had a plan.

At the Hilo airport she rented a car and drove out to National Park Headquarters on the mountain. Most research on the island's volcanic activity was handled by the U.S. Geological Survey, but after various frustrating delays, she finally found someone who knew where the small, private research group had been given permission to set up a headquarters of its own. After navigating a bumpy dirt road well away from the usual tourist area, she arrived to find a small trailer, a metal storage building and various cars and trucks. A helicopter was just landing in a level spot beyond the small encampment.

Cody, wearing baggy, camouflage-type pants and shirt, climbed out of the helicopter alone. The whirling blades slowed, briefly carried along by momentum after the engine shut off. Trisha's first inclination was to dash headlong into his arms, but the fact that he didn't even lift a hand in greeting made her approach at a more cautious walk.

"Anne said you called. I just decided it would be fun...if I came to see the volcano, too." She smiled as she tried to make it sound like a frivolous, impulsive decision, but it came off weak and lame. Awkwardly she added, "But if I'm in the way—"

Behind him a younger man came out of the metal shed and opened the cargo door of the helicopter.

"I must say I'm surprised to see you. I thought you'd be...oh, *busy* today." There was something that sounded meaningfully loaded behind the words, but the meaning escaped her.

"The Pink Turtle was quite busy this morning," she agreed cautiously. "I called my part-time clerk to come and help out this afternoon so I could fly over here."

"You came to the park to meet me for lunch?"

"Of course."

"I see." But it was obvious that there was something he didn't "see" at all, and she felt as bewildered as if they were trying to communicate in some language in which neither was proficient.

"Cody, is something wrong?" she asked bluntly.

He answered with a question of his own. "What could be wrong?"

"You're acting so strangely."

He regarded her unsmilingly for a moment, and then with a long stride closed the space between them. "How's this, then?"

With a dark glitter of blue eyes, he wrapped his arms around her. One hand moved up to tangle in her hair and the other slid down to weld her pelvis against his, crushing her against him until his heartbeat felt like a part of her own. His mouth ground against hers, and his tongue invaded with seductive ruthlessness. She felt a crazy spinning of interior stars, a dizzying whirl of gravity gone awry. When he released her, she stumbled slightly, and he caught her by the shoulders. He looked into her eyes, his head pulled back, as if he perhaps expected a slap across the face.

Finally he asked, "No objections." The words were more challenge than question.

He'd kissed her with deep depths of passion before, but this kiss was different than any he'd ever given her. This time there was a hardness to the passion that matched the blue diamond glitter of his eyes as he waited for her response. She didn't understand this change in him, but she lifted her chin and met the challenge. "No objections." With a lightness she didn't feel, she managed to smile and add, "Except that we do seem to have an audience."

The man who was carrying a bag of something from the metal shed to the helicopter saw Trisha and Cody glance his way and grinned.

"I'd really like to continue this—" Cody's hand slid under her hair and closed around the back of her neck in a harsh grasp that sent tingles shivering down her spine "—but I have work to do."

"You're working with the research team?"

"Just helping out temporarily. The regular helicopter pilot had to make an emergency trip back to the mainland, so I arrived at a convenient time."

"That's why you came over here so...abruptly?"

"Was it abrupt?"

"You checked out of your hotel. As if you didn't plan to return." She hesitated. "Have you decided against buying that building over on Kauai?"

"No." After a brief pause he said, "Kilauea isn't doing much now, but there's been an eruption from a new vent in a remote area. It's a small one, but because it's well outside the area where eruptions have occurred in recent years, it's especially valuable in the research Al is doing. His new equipment, in fact, detected that something was about to happen in the area. Al and one of the other members of the team are staying out there tonight, so I'm going to ferry some camping equipment and food out to them."

All very interesting, Trisha thought, but not exactly *illuminating*.

He glanced at the misty sky and then his watch. "And I'd better get going."

"Perhaps I could...come along?" she asked tentatively.

"I'll also be staying out there all night. It's unlikely there's any danger, but if Al and Warren need to get out in a hurry, I'll be there to evacuate them." His expression changed in some subtle way she couldn't quite interpret. Going thoughtful, perhaps, if she wanted to be generous. Perhaps calculating would be more accurate if she were suspicious or critical. "But I suppose you could come along if you don't mind spending the night."

Trisha hesitated, warnings springing up in her head like stray weeds. She chopped them down with a reminder that this was a research project, not a good-times party, and they wouldn't be alone, anyway. And besides, she rationalized further, she wasn't going to miss the chance to see a volcanic eruption up close. In all likelihood, she was reading something into Cody's expressions or attitude that wasn't there at all; he was probably simply preoccupied with his work here. He must have jumped into it the moment he arrived.

"Yes, I'd like to come along."

Trisha helped Cody and the other man finish loading the helicopter with tents, sleeping bags and food.

"Grab an extra jacket for yourself from the pile in there," Cody said. "Nights are chilly up here."

She hadn't wanted to take time to go back to her apartment to change clothes, so she'd hastily slipped into a disreputable-looking pair of jeans and T-shirt she kept at The Pink Turtle for cleaning jobs. But she hadn't brought a jacket, and here on the mountain the air was indeed much cooler than it was down at sea level. She picked up one of the shapeless jackets colored with camouflage blobs of green and brown that seemed to be the standard uniform here. She was definitely going to be roughing it tonight, she realized. She wasn't certain there was even a comb in her purse.

Moments later, they were in the helicopter, seat belts fastened. The blades whirred overhead, and the craft rocked and danced like some wild creature eager to free itself from captivity. The noise rose to a roaring whine, and the freed craft rose smoothly over the treetops. They headed directly into the rough, roadless area, beneath them a shifting mist that sometimes concealed, sometimes revealed the changing landscape.

Some areas were desolate, ragged with the destruction of old lava flows, but others were green and lush. Trisha couldn't see the main crater of Kilauea, although she was uncertain if that was because of their location or the concealing mist, and Cody was not being particularly communicative. Several miles into the roadless area, Trisha was surprised to see through a rift in the shifting mist a half-dozen people on a slope.

"Who are they?"

"There's an old trail that passes within a half mile or so of the new eruption. It's about a twelve- or fifteen-mile hike from the nearest road, but that group was out there earlier today to see the eruption. It looks as if they're going to camp on the trail for the night."

Trisha gasped when she caught a first glimpse of the red-gold fountain of lava spurting into the sky. Cody had referred to it as a "small" eruption, and perhaps, by volcanologist standards, it was, but that was hardly reassuring. To Trisha it looked as if the world were starting to turn itself inside out.

The molten rock exploded out of a cinder cone it had built around itself, the glowing red lava flowing out of the lower side of the cone. The spurting fountain burned like some barbaric, pagan sacrifice offered to a violent deity, beautiful and savage. Yet there was also a strange delicacy to the fiery display, a dancing grace to the rise and fall of this offering from the earth's interior. The glowing river of lava, narrow at the top where it spewed from the earth, split into wider and slower-moving, multicolored streams farther down the slope. With a turn of the helicopter, perspective shifted, and the fantastic scene was no longer pagan sacrifice but a gaudy diagram of entwined veins and arteries. An occasional tree burst into a torch of flame at the edge of the flow, leaving behind a trail of darkened skeletons.

"The fountain of lava has been varying between seventy-five and a hundred feet high," Cody yelled over the noise of engine and whirling blades. "The lava flow is about a half mile long."

"Is there any danger to people down below?"

"It's still a long way from any inhabited area. But there could be danger if the eruption goes on long enough. Past flows from the big eruptions of Kilauea have destroyed homes and highways and gone all the way to the sea. Al thinks this small one out here will be fairly short-lived, however."

They landed a safe distance away from the eruption, near an area that attested to volcanic activity in the distant past. Lava like black taffy that had risen from some demonic underground and hardened on the surface lay in ropy bulges along the ground. From this point, all that was visible of the eruption was an eerie glow reflected on the mist hovering over the trees. Trisha could feel no heat, but there was an ominous roar in the distance, like that of some enormous furnace, and the acrid smell of sulphur fumes mixed with the smoky scent of burned trees stung her nose. Bits of warm ash settled on her skin. Another helicopter was already on the ground.

Cody immediately started off in the direction of the glow. He didn't invite Trisha along, but he didn't warn her not to come, so she followed. They used the old lava flow as a pathway to the new one, jumping off the ropy bulge where it was overgrown by trees and vines. In one eerie area, she saw devil-breaths of smoke or steam coming up through cracks in the earth. It made the back of her neck prickle. Overhead, she could hear another helicopter circling, but it didn't land, the pilot apparently deciding visibility was too poor to risk landing in the mist that had visibly thickened just in the last few minutes.

"Are the other helicopters part of your research team?" Trisha asked when Cody glanced back once.

"No. We have only the one helicopter. But it's been a busy place today. Researchers from the Volcano Observatory and some other scientists have been out, plus that group of hikers and various newsmen and photographers."

Both cinder cone and red-gold fountain of lava looked larger from the ground than they had from the air, the cone more like a glowing amphitheater framing the devil-spurts of molten rock shooting up from deep within the earth. The scene had a raw, beginning-of-creation look . . . or was it an end-of-the-world omen? The research equipment, otherworldly and alien in this savage environment, added to the strangeness: gleaming surfaces of various-sized metal boxes with busy needles and dials, even something that looked like a small satellite dish. One of the men who was wearing a silvery, outer-space-looking suit for protection edged close to the flow to dip a lava sample. The other man standing farther back, but still much closer than she and Cody were, wore a kind of gas mask that Cody said was for protection from the noxious gases given off by the lava. A couple of photographers were taking video pictures.

Cody introduced Trisha and the two men after they had retreated from the flow—Al Axton, leader of the team, and Warren Devenson. From here Trisha could feel the heat of the lava, which Warren told her was flowing at some two thousand degrees. After a short conference, Cody and Warren decided to hike down the slope and take a look at the front edge of the flow. Trisha, not about to be separated from Cody in this strange, otherworldly place, followed, as did the newsmen.

The front edge of the flow was less spectacular than the exploding red-gold fountain, but it was eerie in the way that it advanced like some eyeless monster creeping over the earth. Here, where the lava had cooled considerably, a thin, dark skin covered the top, broken in places like a wound to show red lava glowing inside. And the strange sound, like the puffing and chuffing of a lumbering locomotive!

After dark, when the eruption looked more gaudy and fantastic than ever, Trisha helped Cody unload the supplies from the helicopter. By then, the other helicopter with the newsmen aboard had lifted off. Cody built a small fire, and Trisha had the coffee and canned chili hot by the time Al and Warren arrived looking for a meal. If her presence here with Cody surprised them, they didn't show it. The conversation during the meal was only about the eruption rate of the flow of lava, height of the fountain, temperatures, content of the gases emitted and a discussion about possible eruptions from other vents in the area.

After the meal, Al and Warren each set up a little pup tent. By now the glow of the eruption filtering through the damp swirls of mist was like an eerie red ghost on the far side of a veil. Al went to bed and Warren went back to keep close watch on the eruption and equipment. They would change places in the middle of the night. Trisha thought that she and Cody would now have an opportunity to talk, but he left to join Warren and did not suggest that she come along. This time she did not follow.

Instead, she sat on a rock and poked at the fire. On the surface nothing seemed drastically abnormal between her and Cody. He was certainly less teasing and affectionate with her than usual, less communicative; he'd seemed more surprised than overjoyed when she'd shown up unexpectedly. But all that was perhaps to be expected when he was in a work environment. When they were walking back to the camp, he had stopped on the old lava flow and kissed her again with that raw passion that made her tingle from fingertips to toes. And yet there was something, a certain wariness or watchfulness about him, that troubled her.

By ten o'clock, when Cody still hadn't returned, she decided to set up her own pup tent. Al was snoring so loudly that Trisha suspected the rumbles might register on the earthquake equipment, and she chose a spot under some trees on the far side of the helicopter to get away from the noise. She spread a sleeping bag inside the small tent.

She heated a pan of water over the fire to wash her face and then made a trip into the bushes. A campsite near an erupting volcano did not come with modern bathroom facilities. It was not a comfortable foray. The mist was almost a rain now, and the wet bushes seemed to take a diabolical pleasure in slapping her in the face and dumping water down her neck. Even with a flashlight she briefly lost her way getting back to camp.

She dried off in front of the campfire for a few minutes and then decided to give up waiting for Cody and go to bed. She left the flashlight on the rock by the fire in case he needed it when he returned.

She took off her jacket and shoes and shoved them into the small tent before kneeling down to crawl inside. The tent had a faintly musty scent and was dark as an old cave. She took off her socks, stuffed them in her shoes and then skimmed the T-shirt over her head. She'd sleep in her bra and panties. She unfastened the zipper on her jeans and squirmed around trying to get out of them. In her squirmings, her hand encountered a bare foot.

It was not *her* foot.

## Chapter Eleven

Trisha squealed and scrambled for the opening of the tent.

"Hey, it's just me." Cody laughed at her momentary fright.

"Cody, what are you doing in here? You scared the hell out of me! This is *my* tent." Yet his presence was not entirely unwelcome. This was more like the old flirty, teasing Cody.

"There are only three tents. You wouldn't have me sleeping out there on the bare ground, catching my death of pneumonia, would you?" he inquired with injured innocence.

"Warren's tent is empty. You can sleep there." She squirmed in reverse, trying to get the damp jeans back to her waist and rezipped.

A strong arm came out of the darkness and pushed her down against the sleeping bag. She struggled like a trapped wildcat until his mouth unerringly found hers in the darkness. That hot, sweet touch stopped her struggles, but for a moment she still resisted with stiffened body and rigid neck. But when his tongue teased her with butterfly flicks and his lips gently drew her lower lip into his mouth, she felt the beginnings of a breathless slide into sweet surrender. His

body slid over hers, pinning her to the ground, and her arms
went around him.

His lips left her mouth but only to rain tender kisses on
her face and throat. They teased the corners of her mouth
and fluttered with dewdrop delicacy on her temples and
eyebrows.

"Cody, I—"

He nipped gently at her ear to silence her weak protest,
and then the tip of his tongue circling the tender curve sent
an unspoken message singing through her. Her arms sent
back a message of their own, winding tighter around his
neck. Cody kissed a closed eyelid, and in the darkness she
saw rainbow shimmers of light.

His hand slid up her rib cage, exploring fingers slipping
beneath her lacy bra and caressing the soft curve of her
breast. She felt yearnings awakening within her, hot, hungry yearnings. And yet her mind still trembled on the edge
of indecision.

"Cody, I—I'm not sure I'm ready to—"

He reversed their positions, putting her on top the lean,
warm length of his body. His arms were still around her, but
it was a loose hold, one from which she could escape if she
chose.

"There, you're free," he announced.

But she didn't want to be free. She didn't want to be free
at all from the magic of this sensuous trap.

"If you think there's a problem," he added, "you could
scream."

She laughed against his lips. "And who's going to hear?
Warren is too far away, and Al wouldn't hear a siren wail-
ing over his snores." And she didn't want to scream any
more than she wanted to be free.

She dipped her head and kissed him leisurely, savoring the
taste of his mouth and the feel of his lips. Just doing that
much wasn't making any irrevocable decision, she rationalized. Her tongue was the invader now, a tentative adven-
turer exploring the differing textures of him with
provocative delight. Hardness of teeth and softness of inner lip, surprising muscular strength of tongue meeting hers.

She was so involved in the kiss that she didn't even feel what his hands were doing on her back until she was suddenly aware that her breasts were no longer confined in their lacy prison. Cody laughed softly with pleasure as he raised her over him and tasted of her ripeness, switching from one side to the other like a gentle predator unable to choose between two equally delightful temptations.

"How come I'm half undressed . . . and you're not?" she challenged recklessly.

"I imagine you could figure out how to correct that situation."

He released her and she straddled his warm body. She fumbled for the buttons on his shirt, undoing them one by one. She knew that somewhere in here there was a point from which there was no turning back, but she didn't stop. At the last button, she pulled the shirt back over his shoulders, and he shrugged out of it. She ran her hands through the soft mat of his chest hair, loving it, loving him. Then he drew her down until naked skin touched naked skin, and she shivered from the delicious pleasure of burying her breasts in that masculine mat.

"Cold?" he whispered.

Oh, no. Not cold. That sweet shiver had nothing to do with cold. She could feel the heat welling up from deep inside her in some hot-blooded parallel to that molten rock welling up from deep inside the earth.

"Do I feel cold to you?" she whispered boldly.

He laughed with her, and then his lips tasted the dampness of her throat and the soft slope of her breasts. With a sudden swift aggression, he reversed their positions. She had never gotten her jeans rezipped, and his hand slipped into the opening and caressed the soft firmness of her abdomen, palm gliding in a circular motion within the feminine curve of her hipbones.

"Is this what you want, Trisha?"

"Oh, yes . . ."

"Last chance to change your mind."

In answer she arched her body in a small circle against his hand, returning the sensuous caress. She tangled her hands in his hair and pulled his face toward hers. With one swift

jerk he could have removed the jeans from her willing body,
but he didn't do it. Instead, the hand stopped midcenter and
the muscles of his neck tightened, holding his mouth poised
a fraction of an inch above hers.

"Desperate situations call for desperate measures, I see."

The statement seemed both odd and irrelevant, but Trisha's mind was in no condition to dissect it for meaning.
Love and desire blended within her like some potent chemical reaction leading to the same pent-up explosiveness of
the volcanic island beneath them. She lifted her head to meet
his mouth.

"You don't have to do this, you know," he said.

She laughed softly. "Are you suggesting again that I
scream?" She gave a breathy squeak. "Sorry. That's the
best I can do."

"No. I'm just suggesting that you don't have to do this.
You don't have to seduce me to get me to buy that building
over on Kauai. The deal is already made."

It took a moment for his words to penetrate the hot fog
of her love and desire. Even then, they momentarily bubbled uselessly in her head. "I don't know what you
mean—" Or perhaps it was only that she desperately did not
want to understand the ugly words.

He unwound her hands, and she could feel him changing
to a sitting position. "Oh, yes, you do. Ever since you found
out I had some money to invest, you've been romancing me
to try to persuade me to buy that building. It turns out your
'old and very dear friend' Hugh is a lot more *dear* than he
is old. And dear old Hugh is in a hell of a financial mess. So
you and he cooked up this scheme to con me into buying the
building and saving his financial hide."

The heat of Trisha's body disappeared in a cold shiver.
What he said wasn't all true. Hugh wasn't "dear" in the intimate, sexual way he implied. But there was enough incriminating truth in his other words to make her swallow
hard with guilt.

"How—" She swallowed again. "Where—"

"I rushed to the broker's office this morning. I had in
mind I'd surprise you with a done deal when we met for
lunch. Along with a couple of other surprises. But *I* got the

surprise. I made an offer. Generally these things go the paper route, but this time the broker made a phone call to his eager seller. Offer accepted. Of course there are still papers to sign and legal formalities to go through, but the deal is made. So you don't have to romance me any longer. I've bought dear Hugh's building. You don't have to seduce me."

"Me seduce you?" Trisha flared. "You were in *my* tent."

Cody ignored that. "But you're probably curious about how I finally caught on, aren't you?" He spoke almost conversationally, as if they were casual business acquaintances having a discussion over cocktails rather than two half-naked almost-lovers sitting on a sleeping bag in a dark tent. "It happened that the broker asked if I'd like to have him start acquiring tenants for the building, and I told him I already had a commitment from The Pink Turtle. Then he said something like, 'Oh, yeah, that's right. Morrison is kicking everybody out so his son can open a restaurant in that building, isn't he?' And this was certainly news to me. You'd never mentioned this small detail that you *had* to get out."

"It was irrelevant. I can find another space for The Pink Turtle. I don't have to have that one."

"So I started to wonder, what else didn't I know? I did know that the owner of the building was rather desperate, given the financial situation surrounding the building. Then another thought occurred to me, one that obviously should have occurred much earlier, given the fact that you had such a one-track mind about my buying that building, and *only* that particular building. Who was this desperate owner? I knew a corporation with the unlikely name of Beachboy Enterprises was the legal owner, but who was behind the corporation? The broker was reluctant to tell me, but I made a few threats about legal investigation, and he decided to reveal to me that the owner was Hugh Lawton, local lawyer. From there, I didn't need diagrams to figure out what you'd been up to. That Hugh's sweet and loving Trisha was willing to give her all to help him, and I do mean *all*, as you've just now proved."

"No..."

"The only thing that confused me was your showing up here today, because I figured the two of you'd be having a big celebration. But then I realized there must have been a slipup and you hadn't gotten the happy word yet, so you were still on the job trying to convince me to buy a building I'd already bought."

Trisha's mind churned. So that was why Hugh had called her this morning with the urgent message that she call him. Not for a progress report, but to give her the good news that the building had been sold.

She shook her head helplessly in the darkness as the truths, half-truths and untruths wound around her like tangled wires. And one truth Cody didn't know, the true depths of Hugh's desperation because of the money he had taken from the estate. Hugh was safe now; the building had sold. But her world was collapsing around her.

"I had a few suspicions about your activities now and then. All those phone calls, and your rushing out in the middle of the night one time after I left you. But obviously I wasn't suspicious enough, or I'd have realized you were carrying on a red-hot, after-hours affair with your real love while you kept me dangling with the innocent act."

Trisha gasped at the harsh mockery in his words and voice. She felt dizzy, disoriented, uncertain which way was up in the dark tent. Something cold touched her hands, and she was startled to realize it was only her own two hands clutching each other.

"Cody, I—" She started to try to explain, to tell him that she had indeed started their relationship with the idea of romancing him into buying the building. But something had happened along the way. She'd fallen in love. But she stopped short as full realization about what was happening here hit her like an avalanche of ice. Cody honestly thought she would make love with him just to entice him to buy the damned building!

She came out of her meek, silent guilt with sudden fury. "You set this up, didn't you? You deliberately set a trap for me—"

"*I* set you up? Oh, come now, Trisha. I didn't beg you to come over here. *You* rushed here in panic because you thought your scheme was going awry. I merely decided that it would be interesting to find out just how desperate you were, just how far you were willing to go to save your dear Hugh. And I found out, didn't I? You're no angel, Trisha, sea or otherwise. Your halo has definitely slipped. But you accomplished what you set out to do. I've bought the building. I'll even lease space to you for The Pink—"

"Cody, you can take your lease and—" She left unspoken what he could do with it. But he undoubtedly didn't need diagrams for that, either. She started grabbing for clothes, but her bra and T-shirt were lost among the wrinkles and folds of the sleeping bag. She found the camouflage jacket and rammed her arms into the sleeves. She grabbed her shoes and crashed headlong through the opening flap of the tent.

He stuck his head out. "Where are you going?"

"To sleep in the helicopter!"

She clambered over the rocks, ouching as her bare feet hit sharp bumps and sticks. Her breath spurted in harsh gasps related more to fury than her wild dash. Once inside the helicopter, she reran the dialogue in the tent like an endless tape.

Yes, the deception had been wrong. She'd admitted that to herself and had wanted to admit it to him. But the idea that she would ever make love with him to persuade him to buy the building was outrageous! Despicable, insulting, degrading, obscene— She ran out of words but not out of anger.

Oh, if she could only pilot the helicopter and leave this very moment! She never wanted to see him again, certainly didn't want to have to share space in the craft with him to get away in the morning.

And she wasn't going to, she decided with fierce determination. She crawled over the front bucket seats to the bench-type seat in the rear. She lay down, pulling the jacket tight around her and determinedly closed her eyes. She needed all the sleep and rest she could get for what she had in mind.

She couldn't stretch out full length, and the jacket didn't provide enough warmth to keep her from shivering occasionally, but she managed to get some sleep. At the first trace of morning light, she put on her shoes and located the purse that she had fortunately left in the helicopter. She stuffed it in a roomy pocket of the jacket and quietly dropped to the ground. She knew approximately where the trail she'd seen the previous day was located. She also knew the going would be rough to reach the trail, but she started out without hesitation. If she kept heading uphill and away from the direction of the eruption, she'd have to run into the trail.

After a half hour of strenuous struggle, she knew that "rough" was an understatement. Trees and bushes and giant ferns, like something out of the age of dinosaurs, grabbed at her hair and face. She tripped over roots and the remnants of ancient lava flows, crawled through low places covered with jungled brush, bumped her head on a low branch. She reached a slope barren of vegetation and started across it, thinking the going would be easier here, but this was a different type of lava, rough, sharp chunks of all sizes. Both her ankles and hands were soon scratched and raw as she clawed her way across the weird jumble of strange rock. The mist swirled around her, making it impossible to chart a course more than a few feet ahead. Sometimes she thought she could hear the roar of the furnace of lava in the distance; other times she thought the noise was only the thunder of her own heartbeat in her ears.

She finally got off the slope of broken lava and back into the trees. But the mist was thicker than ever here. Then up ahead she saw a flash of color. Maybe it was a trail marker... She scrambled toward it, then stopped in shock. The color was oozing out of a raw wound in the earth. Lava! And suddenly she realized that some of the mist swirling around her was rising from the ground, seeping out of cracks. And even as she watched, lava oozed from another vent, like some underground creature testing the surface with a malevolent red tongue.

The stench of sulphur and other acrid volcanic chemicals was almost overpowering, and she remembered Cody warning that a heavy concentration of the gases around an eruption could be lethal. She had wandered into hell, she thought wildly, a hell that she suddenly feared might open up and swallow her. She also remembered Cody's warnings not to go wandering around, but it was a little late now to think perhaps she should have buried her angry pride and waited for him to airlift her out.

Maybe she should go back to the camp— She turned, but she was suddenly uncertain which way she had come or where camp was. Maybe, if she just sat and waited, Cody would come after her....

No. She'd crawl all the way to the sea if she had to, rather than ask for any help from him!

Uphill, she told herself determinedly. The trail was up there somewhere. And if lava started boiling out of the earth, it would run downhill.

Carefully, as if she were walking on the fragile cage of some fire-breathing monster below, she angled to higher ground, skirting a half-dozen smoking vents as if some fiery tentacle of the monster might reach out and grab her.

And then there it was, the trail! An old trail, as Cody had said, narrow, but a freeway compared to what she had just been through. She rested again, mouth and throat dry from exertion. She glanced at her watch. It felt like days since she'd crawled out of the helicopter, but her watch showed only some two and a half hours had elapsed. Would Cody have realized she was gone yet? Not necessarily. He wouldn't be dashing to the helicopter to offer her his magnificent scrambled eggs on a silver platter, she thought a bit sourly.

The trail wasn't a steep rise and fall like the Na Pali trail on Kauai, but neither was it an easy stroll. The mist was lifting, and once she saw a helicopter in the distance, but she couldn't tell if it was Cody's or not. She stopped short when she heard another sound.

"Hey!" she yelled. "Is somebody there?"

She burst over a small rise, as eager to see a human face as if she'd been stranded on an alien planet. The startled-looking faces stared at her as if it were she who was the alien, and she suddenly saw herself through their eyes. Hair disheveled, face scratched, appearing out of nowhere in a strange-looking old camouflage jacket.

"Where in the hell did you come from?" one man asked in amazement.

The story was much too long and complicated to explain. "I just got separated from my...group," Trisha said. "Do you have any water? I'm dying of thirst."

They gave her water and a soggy sandwich left over from the day before. Trisha wolfed it down, not even noticing what kind of sandwich it was. The group was just breaking camp for the return hike out to the road.

Trisha hiked with them. When a helicopter with familiar markings on the side flew in close, she first stepped back under the shadow of a tree where she couldn't be seen. The helicopter turned and flew over the single-file line of hikers again. Reluctantly, the thought occurring to her that Cody might feel obliged to call out some search-and-rescue squad to mount a full-scale search for her, she stepped out where he could see her.

She did not wave, however, and neither did he. The helicopter hovered a moment and then swooped off in the direction of the eruption. If it had been a ground vehicle, she thought, there would definitely have been a squeal of tires.

She trudged on, getting hotter and hotter. Sun had burned the mist away and sweat trickled down her face and back and breasts, but she couldn't take off the camouflage jacket because she had nothing on under it. Explaining the reason for that was a subject she preferred not to discuss with her fellow hikers, so she just smiled and shook her head when one of the women asked if she wasn't terribly hot in the jacket. She dropped to the end of the line so she could now and then surreptitiously lift the material away from her breasts or back for a moment and let cooler air flow across her body. A couple of hours later, she saw the helicopter again, but it did not come in close this time.

She was limp and sweaty, frazzled and footsore by the time the hiking group reached the road and the van they had left parked there. The jacket now felt like a camouflaged steam bath encasing her body. The group helpfully took her to her rental car at the research team's headquarters. Alone in the car, she glanced around to be sure no one was watching and then slipped the jacket off, leaving her upper half bare. She found a nail file in her purse and hacked at the jacket with it, ripping out the lining and tearing off the sleeves. When she put the jacket back on, the unlined material felt rough against her bare breasts, but the nail-file surgery had made a big improvement in weight and warmth of the jacket. But all she could do with her hair was run her fingers through it, and it both felt and looked like frizzled strands of old rope.

The helicopter appeared once more just as she was turning the car from the rough dirt road onto the main highway, Cody apparently checking to see if she'd arrived safely. His duty done, the helicopter zoomed off again. She didn't see any reason for tears...good riddance!...but they trickled down her dirt-smudged face anyway. *Damn you, Cody Malone!*

She turned in the rental car at the airport and was on her way to check the schedules for a flight to Kauai when a hand clamped around her shoulder.

"Going somewhere?" Cody inquired. His tone was pleasant, but it was that dangerous pleasantness of a police officer who has just caught you doing eighty in a forty-mile-an-hour zone. It didn't take much brain work for Trisha to figure out that he'd used the helicopter to get here ahead of her.

"Let go of me!"

"Not until we have a little talk."

"So you can hurl more insults at me? No thanks!"

"We'll just sit down over here—" He propelled her toward a line of chairs by the windows.

"People are staring!" Which was certainly true. Some of the glances were surreptitious, more were open. Trisha could hardly blame them. Dirt smudged her face. Her jeans had ripped knees. Her shoes, hardly meant for hiking over volcanic lava, were almost shredded. The oversize camouflage jacket had ragged edges where she'd chewed off the sleeves with the nail file, and bits of torn lining dangled around her thighs. Cody's camouflage pants and shirt didn't look quite as disreputable as hers, but his face, too, was dirt smudged. A day's growth of dark beard shadowed his jaw and a peculiar smell of volcanic sulphur emanated from him. "They probably think we're a couple of terrorists looking for a place to plant a bomb!''

"Let them stare." Cody flashed a smile at an elderly woman who was indeed staring. "Lovely weather, isn't it?" he said politely.

He let go of Trisha after shoving her into a chair, but he planted himself in front of her as if suspecting she might make a run for it.

"Didn't you care how worried I'd be when you disappeared? At first, I figured you'd gone off in the bushes and couldn't find your way back to camp. I searched around camp for over an hour before it dawned on me that your disappearance was probably no accident."

"How discerning of you. But if you've chased me down just to bawl me out because I didn't leave a note—"

"I also brought you this." He fumbled something out of a pocket in the baggy pants. Her T-shirt, rolled into a bundle. With one lacy cup of her bra dangling brazenly from the roll!

She gasped, looked around to see if anyone was watching... and several people were, with interest. She grabbed the items and stuffed them in her own pocket.

"Thank you," she said, her face redder and hotter than it had been even when she was sweltering in the jacket under the sun. "Now if you'll excuse me, I have a plane to catch. And you might like to check out some fresh lava I saw on my trek to the trail."

"New lava? That's interesting. I'll look into it. But at the moment I have some things to say here." He blocked her way, solid as a camouflaged tank, when she stood up.

"I think you said it all last night!"

"I have some *different* things to say today. And you're going to listen if I have to... tie your feet together with that bra so you can't walk out of here."

A dangerous glint in his eyes told her he was quite capable of carrying out such a preposterous threat. Warily she eased back into the chair.

"I treated you unfairly years ago," he began. "We both know that. And when I figured out that you'd done the same thing to me, pretended a romantic interest with an ulterior motive in mind, I reacted much worse than you did ten years ago.'' He smiled grimly. ''I had my nose and various bones broken in that motorcycle accident, but that's nothing compared to taking a direct hit on the heart.''

Except I wasn't pretending a romantic interest, Trisha cried silently. I fell in love. An irrelevancy from which she would recover, she thought determinedly as she lifted her head and snapped, ''And your oversize male ego was no doubt a bit dented, as well.''

He ignored the comment. ''I'm sorry for what I said and the accusations I made last night. I was mad and...hurting. I know that doesn't justify what I did, but I am sorry.''

''You may be sorry you said it,'' Trisha cut in. ''But you still *believe* that I was actually willing to make love with you just...just over the damned *building.*''

He knelt in front of her. ''No, I don't. I believe you wanted to make love with me because you do love me. That the building had nothing to do with it. Unfortunately, I didn't come to that conclusion until I was stumbling around in the wet bushes, going crazy looking for you, thinking maybe you'd fallen in a vent or God knows what had happened to you.''

''You think my hiking a dozen miles to get away from you proves I *love* you?''

He eyed her thoughtfully. ''Yes, I do. My accusations wouldn't have mattered a damn to you once you'd found out I'm buying the building if you didn't love me. You'd have just shrugged and said, so what? You and Hugh had gotten what you were after. But you *cared.*''

She just yanked a stray piece of lining off the bottom of her jacket.

''Trisha, I intended to come to you with three surprises yesterday. One was that I'd bought the building. The second was that I'd decided either to accept Al's offer to work with his research team, or ask for a transfer from my present job at Mount St. Helens to the Volcano Observatory here.'' She looked up sharply before he even added the last surprise. ''The third was to show up with a ring and ask you to marry me. I don't have the ring...but I'm still asking you to marry me.''

"What about my 'red-hot after-hours affair' with Hugh?" she challenged.

"I care about the future, not the past. I love you, Trisha. And all I can do is tell you again how sorry I am about last night."

A woman's voice announcing that the next interisland flight was leaving in ten minutes came over the loudspeaker. She should be on it—

She swallowed, anger not disappearing but no longer boiling so hot and furious. She knew what it was like to discover you'd been romanced for an ulterior purpose. She'd gone a little crazy, too, ten years ago. Never before or since had she ever attacked anyone with a heavy object.

Hesitantly she said, "Cody, it's true I did start our relationship with the idea of persuading you to buy Hugh's building. I...can't tell you everything even now, but he was desperate, more desperate than you can know. And he *is* simply an old and very dear friend who needed my help. No red-hot after-hours affair. Although I did go to see him late one night when his girlfriend broke up with him, and I was afraid he might turn suicidal." Cody started to say something but she held up a hand to stop him. She'd gotten this far; she may as well tell everything. "You came to Hawaii to find out why I ran out at the reunion. I'm going to tell you why."

"Trisha, that isn't necessary—"

"I ran out because I was *too* attracted to you. Afraid I was going to fall head over heels in love with you, afraid I was going to jump in bed with you that very night. Afraid I'd just get my heart broken again." Suddenly, a flare of anger returned. "And now look what happened!"

"I'm sorry—"

"I don't mean that. I mean that exactly what I was afraid might happen *did* happen. I fell in love with you. And here I am. Hot and tired and dirty, and my feet feel like I've hiked *through* a couple of volcanoes."

"Trisha, I know an apology isn't enough for what I said to you." He stood up and ran a hand distractedly through his hair, releasing another whiff of that strange sulfurish scent. "I guess a man who's in love and hurting like hell does crazy things—"

Like a woman does when she's in love? Trisha thought. Like jumping on a plane and flying off without so much as comb in hand? Like hiking a dozen miles through jungle and old lava? She looked down at her scratched hands. "I should go wash my hands and face—"

He saw her hands, then, and brought them to his lips and kissed the ragged palms, looking at her as if she were in velvet and lace, not a ragged camouflage jacket and torn jeans. "I don't care how you look. All I care about is if you can forgive me. And your answer to my proposal."

Trisha tilted her head. Almost defiantly she said, "I heard something about a ring, but I don't know that I heard any actual formal proposal."

He knelt in front of her, to the interested glances of several onlookers. He didn't seem to notice, much less care. "I've never proposed to anyone before, so I'm not really sure how it's done." He leaned forward and kissed her, not with harsh or seductive passion, not with provocative flirt of tongue or nip of teeth, but simply with sweet tenderness, an invitation not for a moment but a lifetime. "Will you marry me, Trisha Lassiter? I love you."

"I think," she said tremulously, "that that is the way it's done."

She planted her hands on his unshaven jaw and returned the kiss, no longer knowing or caring if they had an audience. Between them flickered heat of sunshine and magic shimmer of moon glow; she saw an explosion of stars behind her closed eyelids, felt a rainbow in her heart and a wild surf pounding in her blood.

"Yes, I'll marry you." She wrapped her arms around his neck almost fiercely. "I love you, Cody Malone."

"But do you forgive me?"

"I think I can manage that."

"Forgive me enough to promise that you'll never ever run away again?" he demanded.

"You ran away, too!"

"So I did. Then I promise, never again."

She nodded her own promise. "Never again."

"Then you and I, my sweet sea angel, have some decisions to make. Large wedding or small? Here or on the mainland? Formal or informal?" His eyes danced. "And about that new bedroom set..."

He went on enumerating choices, happy choices, wonderful choices. But she knew they'd already made the only choice that really mattered. They'd chosen each other.

*     *     *     *     *

**Join award-winning author Marie Ferrarella as she kicks off her new series,**

in May with
**CAUTION: BABY AHEAD,**
**SR#1007**

City slicker Shane Michaels had returned to rustic Wilmington Falls on impulse—and he was *not* a spontaneous man. Country doctor Jeannie Harrigan, too, had been acting quite impetuously. And when their carefully guided paths crossed, their destiny was undeniable—and made in heaven.

Share the wonder of life and love, as angelic babies matchmake the couples who will become their parents, only from

## MILLION DOLLAR SWEEPSTAKES (III)
## AND
## EXTRA BONUS PRIZE DRAWING

**It's our 1000th Silhouette Romance™, and we're celebrating!**

And to say "THANK YOU" to our wonderful readers, we would like to send you a

## FREE AUSTRIAN CRYSTAL BRACELET

This special bracelet truly captures the spirit of CELEBRATION 1000! and is a stunning complement to any outfit! And it can be yours FREE just for enjoying SILHOUETTE ROMANCE™.

## FREE GIFT OFFER

To receive your free gift, complete the certificate according to directions. Be certain to enclose the required number of proofs-of-purchase. Requests must be received no later than August 31, 1994. Please allow 6 to 8 weeks for receipt of order. Offer good while quantities of gifts last. Offer good in U.S. and Canada only.

### *And that's not all! Readers can also enter our...*

## CELEBRATION 1000! SWEEPSTAKES

*In honor of our 1000th SILHOUETTE ROMANCE™, we'd like to award $1000 to a lucky reader!*

As an added value every time you send in a completed offer certificate with the correct amount of proofs-of-purchase, your name will automatically be entered in our CELEBRATION 1000! Sweepstakes. The sweepstakes features a grand prize of $1000. PLUS, 1000 runner-up prizes of a FREE SILHOUETTE ROMANCE™, autographed by one of CELEBRATION 1000!'s special featured authors will be awarded. These volumes are sure to be cherished for years to come, a true commemorative keepsake.

### *DON'T MISS YOUR OPPORTUNITY TO WIN! ENTER NOW!*

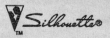

CELOFFER

# IT'S OUR 1000TH SILHOUETTE ROMANCE, AND WE'RE CELEBRATING!

JOIN US FOR A SPECIAL COLLECTION OF LOVE STORIES BY AUTHORS YOU'VE LOVED FOR YEARS, AND NEW FAVORITES YOU'VE JUST DISCOVERED. JOIN THE CELEBRATION...

**April**
REGAN'S PRIDE by **Diana Palmer**
MARRY ME AGAIN by **Suzanne Carey**

**May**
THE BEST IS YET TO BE by **Tracy Sinclair**
CAUTION: BABY AHEAD by **Marie Ferrarella**

**June**
THE BACHELOR PRINCE by **Debbie Macomber**
A ROGUE'S HEART by **Laurie Paige**

**July**
IMPROMPTU BRIDE by **Annette Broadrick**
THE FORGOTTEN HUSBAND by **Elizabeth August**

SILHOUETTE ROMANCE...VIBRANT, FUN AND EMOTIONALLY RICH! TAKE ANOTHER LOOK AT US! AND AS PART OF THE CELEBRATION, READERS CAN RECEIVE A FREE GIFT!

YOU'LL FALL IN LOVE ALL OVER
AGAIN WITH
SILHOUETTE ROMANCE!

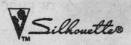

CEL1000

# CELEBRATION 1000! Free Gift Offer

## ORDER INFORMATION:

To receive your free AUSTRIAN CRYSTAL BRACELET, send three original proof-of-purchase coupons from any SILHOUETTE ROMANCE™ title published in April through July 1994 with the Free Gift Certificate completed, plus $1.75 for postage and handling (check or money order—please do not send cash) payable to Silhouette Books CELEBRATION 1000! Offer. Hurry! Quantities are limited.

**FREE GIFT CERTIFICATE**                                                                 096 KBM

Name:_____

Address:_____

City:_____State/Prov.:_____Zip/Postal:_____

Mail this certificate, three proofs-of-purchase and check or money order to CELEBRATION 1000! Offer, Silhouette Books, 3010 Walden Avenue, P.O. Box 9057, Buffalo, NY 14269-9057 *or* P.O. Box 622, Fort Erie, Ontario L2A 5X3. Please allow 4-6 weeks for delivery. Offer expires August 31, 1994.

## PLUS

Every time you submit a completed certificate with the correct number of proofs-of-purchase, you are automatically entered in our CELEBRATION 1000! SWEEPSTAKES to win the GRAND PRIZE of $1000 CASH! PLUS, 1000 runner-up prizes of a FREE Silhouette Romance™, autographed by one of CELEBRATION 1000!'s special featured authors, will be awarded. No purchase or obligation necessary to enter. See below for alternate means of entry and how to obtain complete sweepstakes rules.

### CELEBRATION 1000! SWEEPSTAKES
### NO PURCHASE OR OBLIGATION NECESSARY TO ENTER

You may enter the sweepstakes without taking advantage of the CELEBRATION 1000! FREE GIFT OFFER by hand-printing on a 3" x 5" card (mechanical reproductions are not acceptable) your name and address and mailing it to: CELEBRATION 1000! Sweepstakes, P.O. Box 9057, Buffalo, NY 14269-9057 *or* P.O. Box 622, Fort Erie, Ontario L2A 5X3. Limit: one entry per envelope. Entries must be sent via First Class mail and be received no later than August 31, 1994. No liability is assumed for lost, late or misdirected mail.

Sweepstakes is open to residents of the U.S. (except Puerto Rico) and Canada, 18 years of age or older. All federal, state, provincial, municipal and local laws apply. Offer void wherever prohibited by law. Odds of winning dependent on the number of entries received. For complete rules, send a self-addressed, stamped envelope to: CELEBRATION 1000! Rules, P.O. Box 4200, Blair, NE 68009.

  **ONE PROOF OF PURCHASE**

096KBM

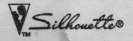